SO CLOSE

TIERNEY BAY BOOK 1

SERENA BELL

JMG
JELSBA
MEDIA
GROUP

Jelsba Media Group

ISBN 978-1-7328948-9-1

Cover and Tierney Bay logo design by Christina Hovland at https://christinahovland.com/

Beach icons by Freepik from www.flaticon.com

Auburn stepped inside Bob's Tavern and surveyed the scene. The left side was packed full of families on vacation—moms with bad sunburns, kids enjoying a rarely-allowed soda, dads relaxed and expansive. The right side was peopled with regulars, and that was where she went: to the bar, where she grabbed two stools and greeted the bartender.

"Hey, Ulysses." Ulysses, a sixty-something ex-hippie with a long, gray ponytail, had been working at Bob's as long as Auburn could remember.

"Hey, kiddo. I heard about Carl. What's the latest?"

Auburn bit her lip at the mention of her beloved boss and surrogate dad. "He's doing great. I visited him at the hospital this afternoon, and he looks so much better. He'll be back to work at Beachcrest in no time."

"It was a heart attack?"

"A mild one. A warning, they said. He needs to make some changes—better diet, more exercise, less stress—you know the drill."

"You tell him that when he feels better he should come by my Monday night Centering with Cannabis group at The Weed

Garden. Best way to de-stress, and now one hundred percent legal."

"Um, will do," Auburn said, hiding a smile. Down-to-earth and relatively strait-laced Carl was not going to take Ulysses up on that invitation any time soon, she knew.

"You holding down the fort at the inn while he's recovering?" She nodded.

"He's lucky to have you. If this had happened six months ago, you woulda still been in New York."

"I know. I'm glad I'm not still in New York. For all the reasons."

"We're glad you're back, too, kiddo," Ulysses said.

Two arms wrapped around Auburn from behind and she turned into her sister's hug. She pressed her face into Chiara's hair, breathing in her comforting apple-cinnamon smell. She would never take Chiara—or pretty much anything in Tierney Bay—for granted again. Even months after returning *home*, it still freaked her out to think that she'd come so close to giving it all up.

"Hey, sis," Chiara murmured, releasing Auburn. "Hey, U," she greeted the bartender, who smiled at her and went back to drying glasses. Turning to Auburn, she said, "How's Carl doing?"

"Much, much better. He'll be out in a couple of days. They think in time for July 4th festivities."

"Thank God," Chiara said. "I'm so glad." She touched her sister's cheek affectionately, then said, "Hey, I gotta run to the restroom. Will you order a drink for me?"

Auburn nodded. "What do you want?"

"Dunno. What are you having?"

"Peach on the Beach."

Chiara grinned. "Not 'sex on the beach?'"

"What is this *sex* of which you speak?"

"Oh, no, no. That is tragic. We've gotta change that, hon."

Auburn scrunched her nose. "Not sure I'm there yet."

Chiara regarded her for a long moment, then shook her head. "Well. Order me one, too. And while I'm gone, check out the hottie at the end of the bar. He could put the sex back in your beach. Or *peach*."

Auburn rolled her eyes at her sister, but once Chiara was gone, she snuck a peek. Her sister hadn't been exaggerating. He was tall, dark, and handsome; broad shouldered; and wearing one hell of an expensive suit. Auburn should know—she'd been all-but-married to a Wall Street hedge fund manager. The guy at the end of the bar knew how to wear a suit, too—he had both the body and the attitude for it. Auburn's girl parts gave a little involuntary shiver. *Not for you*, she reminded them. *We've sworn off guys like that. Permanently.*

Also, who the hell wore a suit in a beach town bar?

She stole one more glance and admired the way the linen hugged him. Custom-tailored to emphasize the power in those shoulders.

Her attention was yanked away by the sound of breaking glass—a tray being dropped. Auburn knew that sound well from years of waiting tables and it was the *worst*. She swung off her stool and went to help.

She didn't know the middle-aged waitress crouched in the midst of broken china and glasses, but she could identify with her forlorn expression. She squatted and the waitress flashed her a panicky expression. "It's only my third night."

"Don't stress, hon." Auburn centered the tray between them and began restacking intact plates and gathering the biggest shards. "I know it sucks. But Johann's super nice. He won't get mad."

"Thank you," the waitress whispered. She grabbed a napkin and began scooping up the spilled food. "And thanks for helping me clean up."

Auburn smiled. "No problem."

Once the tray was reloaded, the waitress thanked Auburn again, and she headed back to her seat at the bar.

"Nice of you," Ulysses said, wiping down her spot.

Auburn blushed. "I just know how it feels."

"Yeah. Well, not everyone would do that." He set a Bob's cardboard coaster on the counter. "What can I get you?"

"Peach on the Beach. Two, actually. One for me, one for Kee."

"On me," a voice pronounced behind her.

She turned to find the hottie. Up close, he smelled unbelievably good—and familiar. Expensive, male, and hyper-competent. Did they put that in a bottle? Apparently so. Plus, she had a love-hate relationship with his bossy self-confidence. Her body loved it and her brain hated it. For good reason, she reminded herself. *Been there, done that, have the scars.*

"It's the twenty-first century, dude," she said. "I think what you meant is, 'Can I buy that drink for you?'"

His slate-gray eyes met hers. "No. I meant, 'The drinks are on me.'"

Really? The size of the balls on this one. She should have guessed. No one looked that good in a suit without being an arrogant prick. Or maybe that was just her post-Patrick trauma talking.

She could feel Ulysses eyeing them both. The glass thunked down harder than usual on the bar's surface. Ulysses didn't approve of the guy's presumptuousness any more than she did.

"Seriously? Who *are* you?" she demanded.

"Trey Xavier. And you are?" His voice was smooth, low, and gorgeous. If it were a drink, she'd order that any day of the week. Plus the purr of it had drawn her eyes to his mouth, which was surprisingly full and soft-looking, considering the rest of him seemed to have been chipped out of a mountain.

But she was done with men who thought they knew what was best for her. What she wanted.

So why were her uncooperative girl parts celebrating him? They'd obviously already forgotten the lesson of Patrick.

Those gray eyes. They were *intense*. Like, he wouldn't take them off her face. He had that alpha male stillness in his features that told her he'd wait forever without filling the empty space with words. And, oh, my God, he was going to devour her with that slate gaze in the meantime. It had been more than six months since she'd had sex with anything other than her favorite toys, and this guy was all sex.

And, oh, he was waiting for her to say something. Right. Her name. What was that again?

She was seven-eighths of the way to remembering and three-quarters of the way to agreeing to whatever he proposed next. Her girl parts knew it and began partying their approval. Getting ready to soak up the whole sensory experience of him, the feel of that stubble on his jaw, which had to be the perfect contrast with the heat and softness of his mouth; the way his scent would concentrate where—

Something clicked in the depths of her brain, and she realized why he smelled so familiar. And the spell broke, just like that. Cracked liked one of those plates the waitress had dropped moments earlier.

"Your cologne costs a thousand dollars a bottle." The words popped out, truth served up cold.

His eyes opened slightly wider. Barely a flinch, but enough to let her know she'd surprised him.

"Asshole ex," she explained. "He wears that stuff. And here's the thing. My ex wasn't the kind of experience I want to repeat. Maybe you guys have nothing more in common than arrogant come-ons and a penchant for suits that cost more than my car, but I really can't chance it. I'm leaving this bar with my sister.

Who's standing right behind you, if you wouldn't mind stepping aside to make room for her—?"

His expression hardly changed. He reached into his pocket and pulled out a leather case and withdrew a business card that he set on the bar beside her freshly poured drink. "I'm staying at Cape House tonight," he murmured. The card was beautiful and obviously expensive. Linen cream. Deeply embossed gold text. For all she knew it *was* gold.

Something shifted in her low belly. *Damn you, girl parts and your taste for alpha men and expensive things.*

She left the card where it was on the bar.

"That's my brother's hotel."

He raised an eyebrow. "Rumor has it the French toast is world class."

She shrugged. That French toast recipe was hers, but she wasn't going to give him the satisfaction of saying so.

"I bet it would taste even better with you sitting across the table from me." He gave a small nod. "You know where to find me." He turned and strode away.

Asshole! And yet, her body reacted contrarily to her brain, because he looked every bit as good going as coming. Those suit pants. That *ass.*

But holy shit, the *nerve!* Who had that kind of nerve? Could you buy *that* in a bottle for a thousand dollars?

"Um, wow?" Chiara said, reclaiming her seat. "He was—kind of like a work of art?"

"If by that you mean look but don't touch, then *yes.*"

Chiara frowned.

"He just invited me to his hotel room. An invitation that apparently included *breakfast.*"

"He—what? And you said no? Do you get propositioned by hot guys so often you can just turn them down?"

"I'm on hiatus."

"Not every guy in a suit is Patrick."

Auburn winced. Chiara knew better than anyone how thoroughly her experience with her controlling ex had messed with her head. "Pretty sure this one is cut from the same cloth. I just don't want to go there. I let Patrick take so much away from me, and I—I almost let him take more." She reached for her sister's hand, and Chiara's expression said she knew Auburn was talking about their own relationship.

"Yes, but now you're back. You have me, you have Levi and Mason and Hannah"—their other siblings—"you have Carl and Beachcrest."

It was a neat little litany of the things Auburn loved, the things she'd almost left behind when she'd gone to New York with Patrick.

"Well, that's exactly it," Auburn said mournfully. "I don't *have* Beachcrest. When Carl retires, assuming I can get the money to buy it from him, yeah, I will. But in the meantime, I don't even have a plan for how I'm going to get that money." That hadn't been part of Chiara's list: lost time. The two years she'd wasted with Patrick in New York, which she could never get back. "So, yeah," she finished. "Until I get some of those pieces in place and feel a little more sure of myself and established here, I don't want to let another man into the picture."

"Okay, I totally get that," Chiara said. "But I'm not so much talking about *the picture* as *the bedroom for a little stress release.* I'm just saying that sometimes having sex with someone else, even if it's meaningless, is a good way to get an ex out of your head."

Patrick wasn't still in her head, was he? "Says the woman who has done that several times with no success."

Chiara's cheeks pinked.

Well, shit. She hadn't meant to be a bitch about it. "I'm sorry. That wasn't fair."

Chiara sighed. "No. But it was completely true."

"Jax and Patrick are two totally different guys."

"Who both turned out to be assholes in the end."

The sisters both exhaled at the same time, then laughed, then hugged.

"Let's just say for a moment that you're right," Auburn said, "and I need to get back on the horse, sex-wise, which is an expression that only women who had their first orgasms riding at twelve should really ever use. *If* that were true, it still wouldn't be that guy." She inclined her head to indicate him. "He's a Patrick clone. You don't get over one rich asshole by fucking another."

Chiara's eyebrow rose. "Patrick's problem isn't that he's rich. It's that he's controlling."

"You mean, the kind of guy who would buy you a drink without asking whether you wanted one and then assume you wanted to know where he was staying?"

"Touché," Chiara said. "But my point holds. Some get-over-Patrick sex wouldn't kill you."

Auburn went to take a drink and discovered that she'd already emptied her glass. She was feeling it, too, a light buzz all over her body. Which was the only reason she peeked down the bar one more time.

Slate gray eyes met hers, and one eyebrow went up. She looked away quickly, but not before her body had time to weigh in. *Yes.*

"Not him," Auburn said. "I just—can't."

Her sister put an arm around her shoulders and squeezed. "Okay. Not him."

Auburn hugged her sister, hard.

As Chiara pulled back, she smoothed Auburn's hair away from her face. "I'm so glad you're back."

"Me too. Have I thanked you lately for rescuing me?"

"Yes," Chiara said. "But I didn't *rescue you*. You rescued yourself. And don't you forget it." She raised her glass and they toasted. "Love you, sis."

"Right back atcha, Ulysses," she called across the bar. "We'll both have another Peach on the Beach, please."

She turned to Chiara and winked. "On me."

IT WAS STILL LIGHT when she walked back to Beachcrest Inn, the golden hour. The sun was setting over the Pacific, and a bank of low clouds had turned shades of pink, peach, and purple. Beachcrest was at the end of a side street, a few blocks from the main drive and the tavern where she and Chiara had spent their evening. Clad in weathered cedar shingle, the inn looked like three houses huddled together for comfort. There were eight guest rooms in the three connected buildings, and two carriage houses—also weathered shingle—held one more room each. It was unprepossessing, which was one of the things Auburn loved most about it. It was so cozy and homey. In fact, it was her home now.

She jogged up the front steps, across the wide front porch with its wicker chairs and swing, and let herself in the front door of the central building, which housed the lobby and front desk. Luz was on duty, a shawl draped over her shoulders.

"How'd it go?" Auburn asked.

"Pretty smoothly."

"No air conditioning breakdowns? No pukers?"

Luz laughed. "Nope. Hey, did you know the group of four checking in tonight were writers?"

"Really?" Auburn said, intrigued. "No!"

"Mmm-hmm. They're here on a retreat ... to write steamy romances."

"Are you *serious*?"

"Yup."

"That's so fun! We have to look them up and get their books. That way, I can at least live vicariously."

"Amen," Luz murmured. "Fictional sex is better than none." She raised an eyebrow in Auburn's direction. "At least you're temporarily celibate by choice. Better than from *lack of choices*."

"You never know. Maybe you'll inspire the next romance. *He* checks in late at night ... *you're* on the desk by yourself ..."

"Is that a love story or a horror movie?" Luz teased. "Anyway, you'll get to meet them at breakfast." She looked at her watch. "Speaking of which, it's late! You have to be up in six hours. You should go the fuck to sleep."

"I gotta get stuff set up for breakfast so I'm not behind in the morning."

Luz shook her head. "I don't know why you don't let someone else do breakfast."

"You know I love breakfast."

"I know you do, babe," Luz said, smiling. "And everything else about this place."

Auburn headed back into the kitchen where she set about prepping everything she could in advance—squeezing the orange juice, cutting the fruit, prepping the dry ingredients for the waffle batter, setting the long dining room table and the smaller tables in the breakfast room. She surveyed the kitchen carefully to make sure she'd done all she could to make her life easier in the morning, then smiled to herself, pleased. She'd made hundreds of breakfasts at Beachcrest during the years she'd worked here—as a teenager, in college, after college—and it never failed to delight her that someone paid her to do this job.

She turned off the lights and headed to the back corner of the house, letting herself into her room with an old-fashioned metal key—not a key card, because Carl didn't like or trust anything modern.

She and Carl both had rooms in Beachcrest. It had been part of the deal he'd made with her when she'd moved back from New York. He wanted her to do full manager duties, but he couldn't afford the salary he thought she deserved, so he'd given her the smallest room, which also happened to be her favorite. It was a corner room with windows on two sides, and even though neither window faced the ocean, the room was flooded with light during the day and looked out over Beachcrest's gardens. Thanks to their longtime housekeeper, Sarah, who did double duty as gardener, the gardens rioted with color all summer long.

Auburn ran her hand over the pretty quilted bedspread, shades of blues and greens, and smiled at the chocolate Sarah had left on her pillow. Sarah didn't clean Auburn's room—she cleaned it herself—but Sarah often left her treats.

There was nothing luxurious about her digs—the room was small, cramped, even—but she loved it more than any place she'd ever lived. And one day, when she saved the money, it would be hers for real.

She sloughed off her clothes, ran hot water in the claw foot tub, then sank down in the water. Her muscles relaxed, even as her nipples tightened at the contrast between the hot water and the cool air. Usually this was where she let her mind wander— over what had gone wrong and right in the running of Beachcrest that day, over what could go better the next. But for whatever reason, as she luxuriated in her bath, her mind kept going back to her interaction at Bob's. Trey Xavier, disturbingly attractive in his expensive suit. And even though she knew it was the *last* thing she should be asking herself, she couldn't help but wonder what she'd be doing right now if she'd let her body, and not her better judgment, steer the evening.

2

"You're a million miles away."

Trey's sister, Brynn, watched him from the passenger seat as he turned off 101. He could feel the power of her stare as he drove.

"Yeah—sorry."

"Work stuff?"

"Yeah," he lied.

It was the best of all guesses, but for once, it wasn't true. He'd been thinking of the woman from the night before. Chastising himself. He'd been impulsive, and he was never impulsive.

On paper, he'd followed the rules he'd made for himself after Karina had left him: No one he knew. No one near home. No one who might tempt him into commitment or a relationship or—in short—no one who'd ever ask anything of him that would pull him away from his business. He preferred to have sex when traveling and he always made it clear that it was a one-time-only thing.

On all those fronts, he had nothing to regret. Last night, he'd been in a town far from home, in a bar, and he'd issued a one-night invitation that didn't pretend to be anything else.

But he knew that he'd violated the *spirit* of the law.

Not because he wanted her. That was harmless and made sense. She was striking and vivid—not his type at all, but hot as fuck all the same. Curls in a riot all over her head, like a kid's impression of a lion's mane. Cobalt blue eyes in a face too cute to be pretty. Generous curves packed into a sports top and leggings, and wedge-heeled flipflops. He'd pictured her naked almost from the get-go.

But that wasn't why he'd walked the length of the bar to buy her a drink.

No. He'd done *that* because she'd helped the waitress.

His mom had worked two or three jobs at a time when he was a kid. Most often, she waited tables or tended bar, and she'd come home with stories for him and Brynn about what it was like. She'd been invisible to most people and used as a punching bag by others. The ones who treated her well were rare. The ones who went out of their way to make her feel human? Practically nonexistent.

Translation: Trey had seen something in the curly-haired woman that he could admire, even *like*. And that was *strictly* against his post-Karina rules of engagement.

He was thankful, now, that she'd turned him down. Well, mostly thankful. He kept seeing the expression on her face during the conversation when she'd lit into him about the cologne. She'd been dead right about the cost. And about him, too. He'd be the first to claim the label "asshole."

And yet, there'd been something behind her eyes as she did it. Interest. No. *Hunger*.

He would have liked to explore it.

"How much further?" his sister asked.

There was a childlike eagerness in her voice. He'd promised her a surprise, and he wasn't the kind of guy who did surprises.

Maybe this was a bad idea, but he couldn't stand for her to stay in that rundown rat hole of a house.

"We're here," he said. "More or less."

He turned down a side street and slowed the rental car—a disappointing mid-size when he would have loved to spring for the Tesla Model S.

"Ta-da."

She slowly pulled herself out of the car and came to stand beside him on the sidewalk, in front of the newly constructed four-bedroom. There was a realtor sign out front, with a sale pending badge slapped across the top.

"What the hell is this?"

"Your new house."

Her eyebrows dove together. "I don't understand."

"It's for you and Jacob and Tyler. I put an offer in on it. I vetted it completely. I know the developer. The builder's very well-regarded. It's good materials, sturdy construction, all new everything." And best of all, a ninety-day closing period, so he could mop up his mess, complete the sale of Home Base, and make this purchase.

There were deep furrows in her forehead. "Why would you do that?"

He raised his eyebrows at the lunacy of that question. "Because you need a better place to live."

"I love where I live, Trey. The boys can walk into town. They can walk to school. When they get a little older they can walk to see Granddad. I love the character and the feel of my home. This place is *sterile*. And way too big for us."

When he'd decided to buy his sister a house, he'd expected some resistance, but he'd thought it would be more along the lines of empty protest. Like, *You shouldn't have. It's too much.* He hadn't expected genuine anger and confusion.

"Your house is a disaster. All the siding on the south side

needs replacing. You're going to have to tear off the deck and rebuild it. The garage is falling down. It's going to end up costing you a fortune."

He could hear his own voice, cool and logical, and he knew: He wasn't managing to say what he needed to say. Again.

Brynn threw up her arms. "Not everything is about money! Jesus, Trey! This is crazy! I know you need something to pour your money into now that Karina's gone, but I can't be that person!"

He didn't move, but something inside him staggered at the blow, and she must have seen it in his face. "Oh God, Trey, I'm so sorry, that was low."

"It's fine. I'm over Karina's leaving."

"It's not, and you're not." She reached out a hand, but dropped it before it touched his arm. He found himself wishing she'd completed the gesture and closed the gap between them.

He shook his head. "This isn't about money. That place isn't good for you. You'll have to work yourself to death just to get by, and you won't be able to get ahead because that thing's a money pit."

Brynn turned away from him. She stood looking at the house for a long time. When she turned back, he could see by the set of her jaw that he was in for a fight. "Look," she said wearily. "For me, this is about getting back on my feet. I broke out of the shitty relationship with Chris, I got a good job that's actually in my field, I bought a place for me and the boys. Is it perfect? Hell, no. But it's ours. And *I did it*. You can understand that, can't you?"

He didn't answer. He didn't *have* an answer. He understood the words coming out of her mouth but not why she would turn down the gift he was offering.

The house stood before them like a reproach. One of five in a cluster of brand new lots tacked on the quiet end of Tierney

Bay's Brideview neighborhood. Peekaboo ocean views. Lots of yard space. Lawns. Two stories, three full baths. Big windows that flooded the interior with light. And she didn't want it. She'd rather live in that rickety, squat little cottage where she and the boys were in each other's hair all the time.

"You really want to help us? Spend time with us. That's what we need from you."

"I—"

She shook her head. Closed her eyes. Opened them again. They were a soft version of his own. "Jesus, Trey, look at you. You're like a deer caught in the headlights."

He tried to protest, but she waved him off.

"I know you're busy. All I'm saying is, you want to help us? Really help us? You can show me and Jacob how to fix the siding and rebuild the deck. You can fly up here every couple weekends and work on it with us."

I work on the weekends. He didn't say it out loud, though; it would just start another argument about how the boys were growing up without getting to know their uncle. She didn't know; she had *no* idea what it took to keep his business running. How he had to be always available, always on. And how even if he did everything right, made smart decisions, the rug could get pulled out from under him at any second, and he'd be right back where he started. His heart raced, something it had been doing ever since he'd learned about the bad investment.

He took a deep breath. No. He was not going to be right back where he'd started. He was not going to let it happen, not on his watch. He was going to do this deal, sell Home Base, and walk away unscathed. And in the meantime, he was going to make sure his sister and her kids were safe and cared for.

"Just let me buy you the house," he said. "It will make your life so much easier. So much better, Brynn. I swear it. I'm not going to be able to spend the kind of time you're picturing to teach you to fix things up at the other place. You have no idea what a time suck that is. An energy suck. It's better this way. This place is ready-made for you and the boys."

She shook her head. "I can't."

God, Brynn was as stubborn as he was. Determined, like their mother. They'd inherited the same genes, just taken different roads.

She crossed her arms. "I won't accept it. You can withdraw the offer or buy the house and rent it or whatever you want to do. But it's not for us."

She didn't have to say, *and you can't make me* the way she would have when they were kids, playing together in the woods. They both knew it was true.

She'd won all their fights back then, too. Maybe because he'd worshipped the ground she walked on then. She was four years older and he'd thought she was a goddess.

Fine. He nodded tightly. "I'll buy it and rent it. No skin off my teeth."

What he meant was, he'd hold onto it until she was reasonable enough to change her mind. She would see. That other place would wear her down. She'd be ready to own this one within a couple of months.

He'd made the same mistake with Brynn as he had last night —he'd tried too hard. Trey Xavier didn't beg for what he wanted. He made the deal impossible to resist, then hung back until people came to him. He could do that in this case, too.

Brynn was looking at him again. "What about the idea of spending some time with the boys and me? At least while you're here for Granddad?"

He hated the note of pleading in his sister's voice. He hated when people wanted more of him than he could give. Like Karina, wanting a night out, a weekend away, an uninterrupted few hours of conversation by candlelight, a piece of him he couldn't spare.

But this was different. It was Brynn, and she was asking him to be her family. To be a better brother and a better uncle. That, he could do. Plus, he had gotten good at parceling himself out in packets just large enough to satisfy the demand at hand.

"I have some time here and there while I'm getting things settled for Granddad," he said reluctantly. "I can visit for a few hours. But once I finish his stuff, I can't be back and forth all the time. I've got this deal I need to finalize."

"Busy, busy, busy," she said. Her voice was almost teasing. Then she got serious—he watched her face go smooth with it. "But Trey, what's it all *for*?"

"What?"

"Why do you do it? The work. The *money*."

She sounded like the voice in his head, the one that had started whispering those insidious things after Karina had left. *Why*? *If she's gone, what's the point*?

"Because I love it," he said.

Her gaze crawled over his face, made him want to squirm. But he held still. Three-quarters of power was keeping your body quiet. Making the other person speak first, move first, act first.

They stood on the sidewalk side by side and he became aware that their postures—crossed arms, set jaws—were perfect mirrors of each other. He dropped his arms to his side, and Brynn did, too.

He turned toward the car, then back toward Brynn. "I can look at the siding with you and the boys tomorrow late afternoon. I've got a conference call in the morning and I'm going to visit Granddad in the hospital in the early afternoon."

Something softened in her face. "Hey." She reached out again, and this time she did touch his arm. "I haven't said, thank you for coming. Granddad really appreciates it. And so do I. I know it's not easy for you to get away from San Fran."

"I came to address the business and financial situation."

"That's why you're here. To—" She quirked her fingers in air quotes. "'Address the business and financial situation.'"

"Yeah."

Her eyebrows went up, and her mouth tilted wryly. She shook her head.

"You just keep telling yourself that."

3

A uburn stopped at the candy machine on her way to Carl's hospital room to buy him a few more packets of peanut M&Ms. It wasn't what the doctor ordered, but she knew her boss, and he'd be going nuts on hospital food. Peanut M&Ms were his favorite guilty pleasure.

As she reached his room, she saw Brynn—Carl's grand-daughter—coming out with both her boys. "Hey," Auburn called out. "How's he doing?"

"Much better," Brynn said, relief painted all over her pretty face. "His cheeks are pink and he looks so much more like himself."

"So good to hear."

"He already has a few packs of those on his nightstand," Brynn said, smiling at Auburn's offering. "I think he's living off them right now. And hey, thank you so much for the casserole. It fed us for two nights."

"How are *you* doing?" Auburn had only really gotten to know Brynn in the last six months, because Brynn had grown up a couple of hours away from Tierney Bay and was ten years older than Auburn. In recent months, though, after Brynn's marriage had ended, she'd moved to be closer to Carl, and Auburn thought they could grow to be friends. Most of Auburn's high school and college friends had long since moved away, and she'd drifted apart from the rest while she was in New York with Patrick.

She couldn't blame them, but she should do something about that, now that she was back and settled in.

"Not too bad, since he's looking perkier," Brynn said. "And my brother's visiting from the SF area, which is—well, a mixed bag—." She cast her gaze up at the ceiling as if pleading for help from above. "—but great for Granddad. He's headed here a little later after some big, important conference call."

"Your brother," Auburn repeated, surprised. She knew Carl had a grandson, but because he was also older than she was— by six years—he'd graduated college shortly after she started working at Beachcrest and she'd never actually met him. He'd visited Carl only a few times, to her knowledge, and never when she'd been around. Carl didn't talk much about him, either; the subject seemed to make him uncomfortable. Auburn vaguely knew that he lived in the San Francisco area and ran a super-successful real estate technology company that had made him extremely rich and very busy. And very distant.

"Yeah. If you stick around more than a few minutes, you might get to meet him. Don't let him sell you anything. Or *buy* you anything."

Auburn raised an eyebrow.

"Long story," Brynn said. She looked at her watch, and alarm flitted across her features. "I gotta run and get Jacob to Tai Kwan Do. Text me later if my granddad needs anything else, okay?"

"Absolutely," Auburn said. "And you text if there's anything I can do for Carl or you or the kids. Or your brother," she added.

"More like, is there anything you can do *about* my brother," Brynn said, rolling her eyes as she left.

Auburn stepped into Carl's room. He did look better. He was sitting up, dispensing peanut M&Ms into his palm, and watching soundless television. "Hey, boss," she said.

He smiled at her. "You're the boss."

It was an old joke between them. Carl said she ran Beachcrest better than anyone else, including him.

"Brought you more of those," she said, and set a new bag on the nightstand. "How are you feeling?"

"Like I need to get out of here before I go postal."

"Brought you these, too," she said, and set two copies of *Games* magazine on his lap.

"Bless you."

"Figured you were probably dying of boredom."

He nodded. "And wondering how you were doing, holding down the fort."

"Don't you worry about me," Auburn said. "I've got it covered."

"I know you do," Carl said. "I don't know what I'd do without you. I don't know what I *did* without you."

She winced.

"That wasn't supposed to make you feel guilty."

"I just wish I hadn't stayed away so long."

"Well. You're here now. Feels so much better to have you back. Beachcrest wasn't the same without you. Sometimes I think you *are* Beachcrest."

Auburn's eyes filled with tears. She knew Carl loved her— but he wasn't the demonstrative type. To hear him say that out loud—it meant a lot to her. It was probably the closest he would ever come to saying *I love you*.

"I think *you're* Beachcrest, Carl. And the place needs you back, so hurry up."

He sighed. Heavily. "My grandkids think it's time for me to retire."

Her stomach tightened. She'd worried this might happen, but she'd tried to think only of Carl's recovery. Beachcrest's future—and hers—needed to be the last of her worries until Carl was healed up. But now he'd brought it up ...

"Do you feel like it is?"

His eyes found hers, uneasy but frank. "To be honest? I do. I was so tired, even before. And the idea of coming back from this and picking up where I left off?" He shook his head. "It was a big relief when I realized they were—giving me permission, I guess. That I *could* retire."

The tears were falling freely now. "Oh, Carl."

His eyes shone, too. "It's hard to say that to you."

"I'm glad you did." She reached out and clasped his big, gnarled hand. They sat for a moment in silence, and then she said, "What will happen to Beachcrest?"

For the first time, he looked away from her, his gaze skittering around.

"Carl?" she asked quietly.

His eyes, a watery gray, came back to rest on her, and she knew she wasn't going to like what he said next, even before he spoke. "My grandson is here."

She raised an eyebrow. "So Brynn said."

"He's come to sell Beachcrest."

Very carefully, she said, "You want to sell?"

Carl drew a deep breath. "I've always thought—*known*—that when it was time, I would sell to you. But—" He closed his eyes, and Auburn's stomach plunged. "Shit," Carl said. "Shit, shit, *shit*."

Don't freak out, she told herself. She opened her eyes to find that there were tears in his, and she started to panic in spite of herself.

"I'm so sorry, Auburn. I should have told you. I tried to tell you."

"Tell me *what*?" she whispered.

"Not long after Sheila died, I got into financial trouble. Bad real estate investments. I couldn't get back on my feet again. While you were in New York—the shit really hit the fan. I was going to lose everything, even Beachcrest."

She'd been with Patrick in New York, half living, when Carl's wife had died. Auburn had come home for the funeral, of course, but then Patrick had laid a trip on her about how much he needed her, and she'd boomeranged back to the city after just a few days. Not long enough to make sure Carl was really doing okay.

Apparently, he hadn't been.

Yet another way Patrick had cost her what mattered.

As if he could see the struggle going on inside her, he shook his head. "It wouldn't have changed anything if you'd been here. No one knew. Brynn only caught on because I needed her signature on an account that had once held her college money—there were a few hundred dollars left in it. That's how bad it was. Anyway, Brynn got her brother—my grandson—involved, and he bailed me out. Took over the mortgage, though he wasn't pleased about it, and he didn't trust me not to fuck it up again. He insisted his name be on the title. So we're—we're co-owners. Officially."

It took a minute for his words to penetrate. Beachcrest didn't belong to Carl. Which meant it wasn't his to give or sell or partially finance or whatever arrangement he'd had in mind all the times he'd said it would be hers one day.

"I meant to tell you right way. I should have told you right away." He was clearly distraught, a few fine beads of sweat breaking out on his forehead.

Quickly she said, "Carl, don't get yourself upset, okay? None of this is worth your health. You're still recovering."

"I am upset, Auburn. I'm upset with myself for not telling you right away, for letting you continue to think that Beachcrest could be yours one day—"

She squeezed his hand between both of hers. "Please don't stress yourself out over this. We can solve this."

Her mind was racing, trying to figure out the implications. Carl's grandson—maybe he would respect his granddad's wishes. Maybe he would hire her to run it. Maybe he would give her time to figure out how to buy it. Maybe this wasn't as bad as it seemed.

But Carl was shaking his head, even though she hadn't said any of it out loud. "He's selling it to a developer. I don't know what the rush is, but he says the purchase and sale has to be inked by right after the 4th of July."

"Developer." Auburn's voice sounded strangely flat, even to her. Raze Beachcrest? The thought made her ache all over. The inn where she'd worked all through high school and college—where she'd found terra firma when everything else had slid out from under her feet. The place she'd imagined she'd one day own and build a future on. And he, this absentee grandson, wanted to build some impersonal hotel or ugly condos? It was bad enough that she might lose Beachcrest, but that it would go away for good, forever? She couldn't—

She couldn't breathe.

"Auburn," Carl said. His eyes met hers, matching pain. "I'm so, so sorry."

"Maybe you could—maybe you could convince your grandson to see it your way?"

"You don't understand, Auburn. He's not that kind of guy." Carl closed his eyes. "He was the sweetest little boy. Biggest heart.

Warmest smile." Grief crossed his face. "He loved everyone. And he loved Beachcrest. But when—when his mother died ... he got tough. Hard. And now he's—it's like he's made of money. I blame myself."

She shook her head, but he brushed off her reassurance. "No. If I could have helped out with things, made life easier for his parents, then maybe he wouldn't be so bitter."

He closed his eyes for a moment, then opened them.

"I'm the one who set him on the business path, too. He used to say he wanted to be a businessman like me when he grew up, so I did his first lemonade stand with him, and then—well, he caught the bug. But I had no idea what he'd turn into. Now he's this Silicon Valley tycoon: all work, no play. When his wife left him, I'm not sure if he even noticed. It's all about more, bigger, power, control. I don't think he cares what the business is, just how much he can sell it for. He's going to sell this one for more than half a billion next month."

"That's what this is about for him? Getting even richer?"

Auburn could hear the distress ricocheting in her own words, but something had distracted Carl, drawing his attention toward the door of the room.

"Well, well, well," said a familiar voice, low and cultured. "We meet again."

4

Seriously? This was the universe's idea of a joke, right? The curly-haired woman sitting at his granddad's bedside, glaring at him like he was something soggy a rat terrier had dropped on her shoes, somehow knew his granddad.

"*This* is your grandson?" She looked back and forth between him and his grandfather, as if desperate to reconcile the two things. Carl and him. Yeah, that wasn't going to happen.

He loved his grandfather, but the two of them couldn't share more than a handful of genes. Unless Carl's knack for losing money and his for accumulating it were two sides of the same coin.

"This is my grandson," Carl affirmed. "Trey Xavier. Trey, this is Auburn Campbell—"

"We've met," Auburn said.

Although technically they hadn't *met*, exactly, because she'd never told him her name. If she *had*, he would have run the other direction because while he didn't know Auburn personally, he knew all about her. She was his grandfather's "adopted daughter," his protege, and the woman—his grandfather had once been fond of saying—who would keep Beachcrest alive after his decrepit bones rotted to dust. As if Beachcrest were an important legacy and not just an overgrown shabby beach shack and two awkward, freestanding cottages trying on "inn" for size.

Thank God she'd turned him down last night. She would have caused him to break the most important rule in his book: never mix business and pleasure.

"You've *met*?" Carl's head was on a swivel.

He was looking a little less elderly today. When Trey had first seen his grandfather shrunken under hospital sheets, it had clawed at some old emotion he'd prefer not to revisit.

"We ran into each other at Bob's last night and Trey offered to buy me a drink." Auburn glared.

She'd looked at him the same way in the bar last night— except last night there'd been something else mixed in. A different kind of challenge in her eyes. Like she wasn't sure if she wanted to fight or fuck.

It had made him want to do both.

"So you know Auburn is Beachcrest's manager."

"I'm starting to get the picture."

"Carl said you're going to sell Beachcrest to some other egotistical, money-hungry 'businessman' who plans to build bland ticky-tacky boxes and sell them to equally unimaginative people." She'd gotten up from her seat and now stood in front of him, arms crossed.

Whoa, okay, so they were going there, and fast. He might quibble with her descriptors, but at least he didn't have to be the bearer of bad news.

"That's right," he said.

He should tell her the whole plan. She obviously genuinely cared for his granddad. If she knew *why* he needed to sell the inn and what was in it for Carl, maybe she'd see things differently. He wished it hadn't taken his grandfather's illness to give him a solution to his own business problems, but he was seriously fucking grateful that the universe had stepped in with an answer when it had. And the fact that he could orchestrate things to leave his grandfather in the best possible situation— that was better than a billion-dollar valuation any day.

"I want to purchase it."

"You want to *purchase* it," he repeated. More to buy himself time than because he hadn't understood. But it *was* incomprehensible to him. He'd stopped by to see it yesterday, as if to reassure himself it was really there, his salvation. The roof had been replaced sometime in the last ten years and the building exteriors looked sound. But the yard was scruffy—grass tufts in sandy soil—and the gardens were overgrown. Probably the word "gardens" was too generous. The rampaging flowers—every shape, color, and height—were an offense to Trey's sense of order; the urge to rummage in the shed for pruning shears and clippers had been almost too fierce to resist. And when he'd gone inside—his fingers had itched with the urge to tear out every last scrap of finish work and put the beach "shabby chic" furnishings out on the curbside for pickup.

"Yes. I want to buy it from you."

Her arms were crossed, pushing her tits up. He'd fantasized about palming those curves last night while he helped himself to the crush of his fist, and he'd come in fewer than ten strokes.

That was when he'd still been deluding himself that he'd ever lay hands on those breasts. They were a long way from *that* right now, and if she thought she was going to buy Beachcrest, they were about to be a lot further away still.

"I promised to sell her Beachcrest when I retired. That was the plan, before your grandmother died," Carl said.

Trey wasn't surprised. Of course he fucking had. That was Carl for you, impulsive and impractical. He turned on his grandfather. "You shouldn't have done that."

"It was before you bought in—"

"Then you should have told me that you'd made a promise you couldn't keep. And you should have told her the truth, right away when I bailed you out and we added me to the title. That you didn't have the right to make that decision anymore." He turned to Auburn. "I'm not the bad guy here, I'm just making the best business decision."

"You're making the best business decision for *you*," Auburn said. "You're not making the best business decision for Beachcrest, because it will cease to *be* a business if you have your way. And maybe he should have told me, but he didn't." She squared her shoulders. "Now I know. And I can't just let you sell it to someone who wants to tear it down."

She was gutsy, he'd give her that. She didn't flinch or back down. Her eye contact didn't even waver. He'd have to shut this down right away. He needed this sale, and he needed it to be quick and easy.

"What are you going to do to stop me, exactly?"

For the first time, he saw uncertainty in her gaze. She bit her lip, a pearl of white digging into the soft red flesh. "I told you. I'm going to buy it."

Oh, sweetheart, you have no *idea who you're dealing with.*

"And why would I sell it to you?"

She cast a look Carl's way.

"Because I love Beachcrest. I've poured myself into it."

"She *has*," Carl jumped in. "No one works harder than Auburn for Beachcrest. Not even me. No one knows Beachcrest better. No one understands its magic as well."

"Magic," he said, scornfully.

Auburn, who had stood straighter during Carl's speech, turned hard eyes on him now. "Yes, magic," she said. "It's an amazing place. It brings people together. It changes lives."

He rolled his eyes at that. If Beachcrest was magic, he was fucking Dumbledore.

She'd opened her mouth to say more, but he cut her off. "Do you have the money to buy it?"

"Not yet—but I can get it," she said eagerly.

He felt the weight of some unexpected emotion, and then he realized: It was disappointment in her. She was just a goofy idealist, and he'd thought she was going to put up a real fight. As much as he didn't want complications—as much as he couldn't afford any delays, he'd been *excited* by the idea of sparring with her.

How long had it been since he'd been excited about anything?

Since long before Karina had walked away.

Longer than that.

"Don't bother."

All the eagerness on her face fell away, and for a split second he wanted to reach out, like he could somehow stop it before it faded. Then her glare was back. That was better. He liked her best that way—all her defenses up against him. No chance for anything like a detente. This wasn't a game, anyway. He had a deal to make, and he wanted to get it done, not joust with a girl who believed in *magic*. He'd packed up his wands and spell book by the time he'd made his first sale, which was at the age of five, thank-you-very-much.

"You're a cold-hearted bastard," she said.

He didn't let himself look at his grandfather. He didn't let himself question why he'd chosen not to explain himself.

"Yes," he said. "I am. But I believe I gave you my business card? Feel free to call me when you've managed to get your hands on a down payment for a multi-million dollar sale. Until then, I have other matters I need to attend to."

And ignoring her expression of disbelief, he turned on his heel and walked out of the room.

5

"I'm going to lose Beachcrest."

Chiara rubbed Auburn's back in small, comforting circles. "You're *not* going to lose it."

Auburn's face was buried in her hands. After her showdown with Trey Xavier in Carl's hospital room that afternoon, she and Chiara were sitting on Auburn's bed, doing justice to a bottle of Oregon Pinot.

"You don't understand. This guy isn't going to budge. He doesn't have a budging bone in his body."

"I got that feeling, looking at him," Chiara said dryly.

"Don't joke. I shouldn't have pissed him off in the bar."

"What should you have done? Slept with him so he'd give you Beachcrest? Just think how much more of a mess this would be now if you'd done that."

"God, yes, that would be a goat fuck. But—did I have to make him hate me?"

"From what you've said, he would have been a dick about this anyway."

"Probably." Auburn sighed.

"Did you talk to the lawyer?"

"Yeah. Carl can't sell Beachcrest without Trey's buy-in, which sucks. The good news is that Trey also can't do anything without Carl's buy-in. So they have to meet in the middle."

"That's good for you, right?"

Auburn shook her head. "Carl just had a heart attack. He's seventy-one years old and ready to retire. And it's *Carl*. I love Carl. I don't want to put him in the middle of this. And I really don't want to make him pick between me and his grandson—"

"He'll pick you."

Auburn shook her head. "That's not the point. He loves Trey. You should hear the way he talks about Trey when he was little. The sun rose and shone on that boy, that was for sure. I'm not going to ask him to screw his grandson over. Not even for Beachcrest. So I think I might be shit out of luck. Maybe I should look into getting a real estate license so I can sell those fancy new condos of Trey's."

Her sister's face was full of sympathy. "I'm pouring you more wine."

Auburn took a healthy swig, leaned against the white upholstered headboard, and gave in, for a moment, to despair.

"Have you tried explaining to Trey why you love it so much?" Chiara asked.

Auburn shook her head. "I tried, but I just kind of babbled about magic, and he was disgusted. I didn't tell him any of the real stuff. About how when Mom and Dad died, and you were at college—"

It was hard to talk about. How Levi had been busy trying to save them all. Hannah had been drowning in her own grief. And Mason had been as remote as ever. Untouchable. Unreachable.

Beachcrest had been an island of calm, a place where people went to be joyful. Carl and his wife had been her oasis and working there had given her purpose. She could create a magical experience for vacationers, even if her own life was full of pain. In the kitchen, there was peace—the rhythms of chopping, beating, stirring. In the dining room, there were the distractions of conversations with people from all over the world. There were the glimmering moments—two friends who hadn't seen each other since high school, reunited. An engagement on the beach. A sixtieth wedding anniversary.

She shook her head. "Even if I could explain it, he's not going to get it."

"Maybe—?"

"He's a bean counter, Chiara. A ones and zeroes guy. Beachcrest is the opposite of that. It's all peopley and warm and fuzzy. It's like he and I exist on parallel planes of the universe."

Auburn's phone vibrated. She leaned forward and flipped it over.

"It's Carl," she said, feeling a tiny buzz of hope. "He says to call him. He wants to talk about the Beachcrest sale."

"Do it," Chiara said. She poured herself another glass of wine. "Do you want some privacy? I can go out to the lobby."

"No. Stay."

Auburn tapped to make the call.

"Hello?"

"Hey, boss." Carl's gruff tones filled her ear. "I need you to do something for me."

"What's that?"

"You're like a daughter to me, Auburn. Or another granddaughter. Whatever you want to call it."

Tears filled her eyes.

"And Beachcrest is my life's work. I've had my ups and downs, I told you, but Beachcrest is the one thing I've done right. I can't see it torn down, Auburn. I can't. I want to fight Trey. I want to sell it to you, and then I'll know you have it and will take care of it for me."

The tears ran down her face, but she swiped them away and

took a deep breath. What he was offering—she wanted so badly to reach out and grab it, but—she had to keep Carl at the forefront of her mind in all this. Beachcrest was important, sure, but it was a thing, not a person. And Carl was sick, and tired, and old. "Trey doesn't seem like an easy person to fight, Carl. Taking him on would be complicated and exhausting for you. And as your surrogate daughter or granddaughter or whatever I am, I can't condone your fighting him when you're also trying to recover from a heart attack."

He sighed. "Yeah. I knew you'd say that. Here's the thing, Auburn. I'm going to do it whether or not you condone it and with or without your help. It's just a question of whether I have to make all the lawyer phone calls and have all the ugly conversations myself, or whether you're in it with me. None of this would be happening if I hadn't fucked up—"

"Don't," Auburn said quickly. "Carl, please don't. We all make mistakes."

He exhaled heavily. "I made a mistake with the rest of your life, Auburn."

"I will figure out the rest of my life, Carl. You don't have to do penance. And you don't owe me anything. You've given me so much already."

"It's not just you, boss. I can't hand Beachcrest over to be torn down. It's *my* home. And I can't just let some butt-ugly condos get built there. It'll be a blight on the whole beach."

She sucked in a breath.

"See, you agree. If you won't do it for me, Auburn, do it for Tierney Bay."

She smiled at that. "Carl. You know I would do *anything* for you."

"Then I'm telling him I refuse to sell Beachcrest to a developer. I'm selling it to you."

She looked around her room—the popcorn walls, the

distressed white furniture that had been so fashionable when Carl had last redone the rooms, the drapes that Sarah kept clean and ironed but that were starting to show wear. *This* was where she belonged. Beachcrest was home.

And it was where Carl belonged, too, in his retirement. If Trey prevailed, Carl would lose not only his legacy but also his *home*. If she fought for him, with him, the room he occupied now could be his as long as he wanted it.

She took a deep breath. "Carl—are you sure? This isn't going to be an easy fight, and you're supposed to be getting your strength back."

"Sure as I've ever been of anything."

"You know I don't have the money. Yet."

"Auburn Campbell, I've known you your whole life. You'll find a way to get it."

She wished she were as sure as he was, but his faith warmed her.

"He's supposed to show up around two tomorrow. Why don't you plan to come at two fifteen? That way I can have a few minutes to talk to him alone, but you can swoop in as my backup."

She hesitated again. But he'd been more than clear. She'd given him every out. And—well, he wanted what she wanted.

"You got it, boss."

"You're the boss."

She closed her eyes to hold back tears, ended the call, and turned back to Chiara.

"Ready to roll up your sleeves?" she asked her sister, who was watching her intently.

Chiara grinned. "Hell yes. Trey Xavier isn't the only stubborn ass in Tierney Bay."

6

"Seriously? You would do this to me? Your own grandson?" Trey had to work hard to hold his voice to a hospital room-appropriate volume.

Carl sat up straighter in the bed. "I'm not *doing* anything to you. You and I are just two co-owners who disagree about next steps."

"Bullshit. You're keeping me from doing the smart thing with a piece of property that you forfeited your right to care about. When you threw good money after bad, Beachcrest became my responsibility."

Carl took a deep breath. "I know when you had to come bail me out, you were very disappointed in me—"

Trey didn't have time to listen to his grandfather's pop psych crap. "No, I was just irritated to have to take time off work to solve your problems."

His grandfather flinched. Trey knew he was a dick to fight with a seventy-one-year-old man consigned to a hospital bed. But this conversation had been a long time coming, and he couldn't let Carl be snowed by a pretty girl who believed in magic.

"I know you wanted me to be different from your dad."

Yeah, he had. Carl had taught Trey everything he knew about business. And he'd flat out told Trey it was because he needed a role model who was better than his own father. Someone who didn't act on impulse and throw away everything decent he got his hands on. But in the end, Carl had turned out to be cut from the same cloth as his son-in-law.

"Did *she* put you up to this?"

He could see Auburn in his head, fierce, stubborn, arms crossed, and he felt a twinge of something that wasn't quite anger. He wished he could un-see her the way he first had—the woman who'd knelt to help a waitress, the standout in a bar full of pretty girls, a spitfire he'd wanted to spar with as much as he'd wanted to take her home. That image kept getting in the way of what he should be feeling, which was straight-up, pure fury at the way she was thwarting his plans and putting his future at risk. Undoing everything he'd worked for.

His grandfather shook his head. "No. It's what I want. Tierney Bay doesn't need luxury condos. It needs a personal touch, a place that feels like home to people."

What if he just laid it out? Explained why he needed the sale? Explained the situation he'd gotten himself into—

Explained that he was really no better than his father or his grandfather?

But he *was* better. He had an escape plan. There was a way out, a way forward, and all he needed to do was remove one curvy obstacle from his otherwise straight path.

Trey shook his head. "So you're serious about this. Keeping me from making this deal."

"If you want to put it that way," Carl said. "I prefer to think of it as encouraging you to make the right deal."

He'd forgotten his grandfather had a stubborn streak, too. And at that moment Carl was cool as a cucumber, and Trey was not—which knocked him off his game. He took a deep breath. "You know this means I have to get a lawyer involved. And if I do, it's going to be expensive, and I'll probably win in the end."

He was bluffing the fuck out of the situation. Because he didn't have time for lawyers. But they didn't know that. And they didn't know that time was on their side, that even though he would force the sale eventually, he couldn't afford *eventually*.

Carl nodded.

"I don't fucking understand."

"No. That doesn't surprise me."

Suddenly he'd had enough. He turned and strode out of the room, and nearly collided with someone. Someone soft and curvy. He grabbed her to steady her, but failed to prevent the collision of her breasts with his chest. Her arms were bare, soft and satiny in exactly the way he'd imagined.

Enemies should not smell this good or feel this soft.

So. Goddamn. Inconvenient.

"You," he said darkly. "Are you having fun cock-blocking me?"

"I could ask you if you're having fun being a cock," she snapped. "But if you must know, no. This isn't my idea of a good time."

"I bet you haven't had a good time in your life, sweetheart," he shot back. "And things are going to get a whole lot less fun if you keep fighting me. The fact remains, you have no money. And you have no idea who you're dealing with. At the end of the day, you're going to make all our lives miserable, and you're still going to lose Beachcrest."

"I'll get the money."

"I'm calling my lawyer," he said. "I don't know how much experience you have with lawyers, but they change everything. Right now, we're three people who can talk this out like civilized adults. Once there are lawyers involved, things are going to move fast. You're not ready for just how fast. And Carl owns far less than half of Beachcrest."

He saw the flicker of anxiety behind her eyes, but she pulled herself up to her full height and stared him down, that flicker vanishing into cobalt blue conviction. He felt a flare of heat in his chest. It might have been anger—or something else.

"I wouldn't fight you if it was just me," she said. "Beachcrest means more to the people of this community and the people who come to stay here than you give it credit for. This is what Carl wants. And Carl has been there for me my whole life. After my parents died. When I came home again after—"

She stopped. Her eyes found his. "I won't give up until Carl tells me he surrenders. Which he won't."

She stepped neatly around him and continued down the hall to his grandfather's room. And he found himself standing alone in the hospital hallway, the feel of her arms still soft and hot against his empty palms.

7

"He's right," Auburn told Chiara later that evening. They were eating Tierney Bay diner takeout in the Beachcrest dining room. In the breakfast area next door, the romance authors were having some kind of plotting session. Periodically, a few words would burst into audibility. *Blow job. Hot mess. HEA.* They were obviously having a lot more fun than Auburn and Chiara were.

"If I don't have the money, I'm just making his life miserable for no reason. Not that he doesn't deserve it."

Running into him had felt like colliding with a solid wall of muscle. He hadn't been wearing Patrick's cologne this time. Something else, something spicy and musky that had lowered her IQ by a hundred points. She was so irritated with her monkey self, she could shake it. She was a grown woman with a big brain and plenty of self-control—

Except when he gave her that look. The one she couldn't read. She'd swear he wanted to throttle her, but the look said he wanted to push her against the wall and kiss her until both of them were breathless.

What was she supposed to do with that?

Nothing. She was supposed to do *nothing*. She was supposed to plant her feet and stand her ground, and ignore her howling, hooting bonobo self.

"You're going to get the money," Chiara said. "Do you know what price he'd accept from you?"

"Carl and I are getting a going-concern appraisal on it, so I'll know soon. But it's going to be—" She took a breath, because she knew the number would sit with Chiara about as well as it had with her. "Probably three to five million. A down payment of at least several hundred thousand, if not more."

Chiara drew her own sharp breath, and the sisters sat for a moment with the truth of it.

"So what are your options?"

"Convincing a lender to give me financing with little or no down payment."

"Yeah," Chiara said. She didn't sound any more optimistic about that than Auburn felt.

Auburn speared another tender bite of steak. Lily—the co-owner of the diner—could *cook*. "Or. Getting a loan for the down payment. I could ask Levi."

Chiara nodded. "You should definitely talk to him."

"There's Patrick."

Chiara winced. "*Really*?"

"No. I just had to put it out there. But no."

Chiara had been the first person brave enough to tell Auburn she didn't like or trust Patrick. In the end, Auburn had almost lost Chiara over it, but her sister had been too loving and stubborn to let Auburn slip away.

God, she loved her.

"When I walked away, he said, 'If you ever need anything money can buy, you know where to find me.'"

"Who the fuck makes those his parting words? I hope you flipped him the bird as you walked out of his life forever and said, 'Freedom doesn't cost a thing, motherfucker!' Even Beachcrest isn't worth stooping to that level."

"At the time, I said, 'I will NEVER ask for your money.' And that goes double now, especially since he's still leaving me messages saying he wants to *talk*."

They both winced at that, and Auburn looked away. Given what he'd done to her, there was no chance she'd let Patrick back into her life, which meant she couldn't afford to take his money. Even if he was made of it.

"You could use one of the cloud-sourcing sites, like Bootstrap."

"Would Bootstrap work for something like this? This is a shit-ton of money we're talking about, and what kind of stake could I really give people in it?"

"Free one-night stays," Chiara said. "Plus, that would be a terrific loss-leader, because who wants one night? People would redeem their free stays and then spend a few nights."

Auburn tilted her head. "It seems like a long shot."

"It's worth a try. I can sit down with you and help you figure out how to set it up."

"That would be amazing. And in the meantime, I'll talk to Levi and the banks, I guess."

Chiara leaned over and gave her sister a hug. "If I can help, I want to."

"You're helping by listening." There was no way Auburn would take a penny of her sister's hard-earned money.

Auburn sucked down a slug of root beer. Another thing Tierney Bay Diner did right—served an amazing locally brewed root beer.

"Aub?"

"Mmm-hmm?"

"Why did you take Trey's business card home?"

Startled, Auburn caught her sister's knowing gaze and felt herself blushing to the hairline.

"I didn't think you saw that." She'd grabbed it behind Chiara's back as they'd walked out of the bar. Because. Because it was beautiful and so was he, and even if she had no intention of doing anything about it, she couldn't quite bear to leave behind the evidence that he wanted her. "Anyway, it's moot. No way I could possibly have sex with him *now*."

"Well, it might help convince him to sell you Beachcrest," Chiara said playfully.

"I would *never* sleep with someone to get something from them. Never." Auburn's voice cut right across her sister's teasing, steely.

And more than a little defensive.

Her stomach hurt, suddenly.

"Never again, anyway," she said quietly, finding her sister's gaze.

Chiara raised her eyebrows and put a hand on her sister's knee. "It wasn't like that. You know that, right? You weren't Patrick's...mistress."

Auburn set her root beer down on the coffee table. She took a deep breath. Mistress was nicer than the word that had flitted through her own head during Chiara's long pause.

"Maybe so—but it was sure how it felt, in the end. I promised myself that I'd never let anyone own my life like that again. And since my life *is* Beachcrest at the moment, that means I can't let anyone take it from me."

She took a deep breath and squared her shoulders.

"I'm here to win."

8

T rey's nephews, Tyler and Jacob, stood on either side of him as he tapped another nail into the siding of Brynn's house. "You don't want to drive the nailheads flush with the siding. Because the head will break the face and let water in."

He showed them how to leave just the nailhead exposed, then handed the hammer to Tyler and watched him as he imitated what his uncle had just demonstrated.

"Good," Trey said.

Tyler had gotten a lot more comfortable with the hammer over the last few days.

Helping his nephews reminded Trey of when Carl had shown him how to build the covered lemonade stand. That had been his favorite part of the whole venture. Aside from counting the money at the end, of course.

Working with Tyler was pretty satisfying. The boy was a good listener and a hard worker. So far, they'd cut away the rotted siding, primed and painted the new boards, and begun replacing the ruined pieces. Next they'd caulk any gaps.

You could see that Tyler was eager to be helpful to his mom.

Trey remembered the feeling well. Wanting to be helpful was how Trey's first *real* business had gotten started. He'd done so much yardwork for his mom that it had made sense to start charging other people to do it. Xavier Landscaping had eventually grown more successful and better trusted than most of the companies run by the town's men.

Brynn came up beside him. "Thank you," she said quietly, tilting her head to indicate her son.

"I'm here anyway, until I get this deal done."

"You can't just say *you're welcome*, can you."

It wasn't a question, so he didn't try to answer it.

"What's going on with the inn? I thought you were selling it to your developer friend?"

"Things got a little complicated. Auburn Campbell wants to buy it."

The mention of her name set his blood in motion. *Just anger*, he told himself, though he knew it was a lie.

"Huh," Brynn said. "And you're thinking about selling it to her?"

He didn't like the mischief in Brynn's eyes. This wasn't some kind of joke or game. It was a time-sucking pain-in-the-ass. He was letting the bluff sink in for his grandfather and Auburn. A long legal fight they'd almost certainly lose. He'd be willing to bet they'd talked to their own lawyers by now and were just about ready to back down.

"No. Absolutely not. But I can't sell it to my developer contact without Carl's buy-in, and he can't sell it to Auburn without my buy-in."

"Interesting," Brynn said, dragging the word out to a thousand syllables.

He ignored her, pointing at the house. "When you water the lawns, you need to make sure no water hits the house. Or you'll get more rot."

His phone rang.

"Can you watch Tyler with the hammer for a sec?" he asked Brynn. "And then make sure he helps Jakey hammer one in, too?" He stepped away to answer the call. "Xavier."

"Hey, Trey, it's Doug. Rumor has it things aren't going as smoothly as you'd like on the Beachcrest front."

Trey let his head fall back, his eyes closed. "Who've you been talking to?"

"Hey, man, I grew up in that town. You know I have ears there. Someone mentioned to someone who mentioned to someone that the woman who's been running the place for your granddad wants to buy it and your granddad is on board with selling it to her. And also that she has *no fucking money*."

"I've got it under control."

"Jesus, Xav, I hope you do. There are a hundred and fifty employees here who hope you do. We don't have time to dick around. It's shit or get off the pot time."

"I know that," he said tightly.

"If you're not going to do the deal, I've got to get these severance packages paid out—"

"I *know*."

The tightness in his voice must have finally gotten through to his chief operating officer, because Doug sighed. "I hope you do. You know a partition suit could take weeks. Months."

"They don't know I'm in a hurry. They're going to lose if it goes to court. Their lawyers will tell them that, and they'll back down. I give it less than twenty-four hours."

"What about the woman? Can't you offer her something that'll make her go away? Everyone has a price."

He hadn't tried to buy her off outright. But he'd seen the conviction in her eyes. Still, Doug was right. If there was a sum he could offer her, he had to try. They could pay it out to her once the Beachcrest deal was done. She had to have a weakness. Maybe her family ...

"Don't worry," he told Doug. "I've got it covered. You sit tight, I'll take care of business here, and you'll get your bonus when Home Base sells."

"Your mouth, God's ear," Doug said, but he sounded a lot less certain than Trey would have liked.

He ended the call and stepped back to where Brynn stood.

"Hey," she said. "Since you have to be here anyway, what if I made you dinner tonight?"

"I, um, have to deal with something at Beachcrest."

It was always better to have a tricky conversation in person if you could.

What was it Brynn had said to him the other day?

You just keep telling yourself that.

9

"Oh, God, we're losing South America," Auburn said. "Deja, can you get down there and do something?"

Chiara, Auburn, and the four romance writer guests were playing the board game Pandemic in the dining room of Beachcrest—cooperatively trying to save the world from four deadly diseases. Between them, the romance writers had brought nearly an extra suitcase's worth of card and board games with them on their retreat, and they'd roped the sisters into an evening of pizza and play. It was the first time since Carl's heart attack that Auburn could remember laughing and having fun.

"By the time I can get there, we're going to have at least one more outbreak," Deja said. She was the oldest of the women, her bright pink afro poking up above a vivid orange and yellow scarf. She was also the organizer of the retreat that had brought them to Beachcrest for two weeks of writing, eating, shopping, and beach walks. "I think Aria has to go."

"But you have the fast-treating ability, so you can save more people once you're there," Aria protested, tossing her candy-floss blond hair.

"Which won't help us if we're dead," Deja countered.

The front door chime sounded.

"Do you have to get that?"

"I should," Auburn said. No one new was expected that night, so it was probably just one of the guests coming back. She pushed her chair back, but before she could stand, she heard footsteps coming toward them and saw Trey's tall, broad form appear in the doorway, blocking light from the lobby.

"Well, hello," Aria said, delightedly, to the newcomer. "Come in. Make yourself at home. Turn in circles a few times so we can all admire you."

"Do you verbalize every thought in your head?" demanded Priya, whose black hair was bound up in a big-mouthed hair clip.

"When sex manifests in the flesh, yes," Aria said unapologetically.

The look on Trey's face nearly made the last few days worth it. Auburn had never seen him caught off guard, and right then he looked like a hamster tossed into a rattlesnake cage. Then the mask descended again. "Hello, ladies." No smile, of course, but his voice was as smooth as good gravy. "A word," he said to Auburn.

"Are you asking to speak with me? You could try, 'Hey, sorry I'm interrupting, but when you get a minute, could we talk?'"

Trey's eyes blazed, setting up an answering heat in her low belly. A volley of glances went around the table.

"I said what I meant," he said, his voice a thousand degrees cooler than his eyes. "But I can translate it if it'll make you feel better. When you get a minute, I'd like a word."

He'd twisted her words to take the request out of them, of course.

"Fine." She didn't get up, mainly because she knew it would

drive him nuts. If she was going to lose Beachcrest, she was going down swinging.

"*Alone?*"

"Anything you need to say you can say with these ladies present."

Hesitation flitted across his features, so briefly that she wasn't sure if she'd imagined it. And she must have, because Trey Xavier surely didn't hesitate over, well, anything. "I'm filing a lawsuit to force the sale of Beachcrest."

A chorus of gasps rose around Auburn. She'd known it was coming, but it made her heart pound. Still, she wasn't going to let him know she was shaken. "Ladies, allow me to introduce Trey Xavier, the man who wants to replace your writing space with condos. Maybe he'll be nice enough to let you rent one for your next gathering. I'm sure you'll find it as inspiring as Beachcrest," she told her audience. She knew how guys like Trey worked. She'd been with one for years, had listened to more than her share of one-sided phone negotiations. Those with the largest—er, sexual organs—won the day. She turned to face him. "I lawyered up, too, Trey, and a lawsuit is going to be a pain in the ass for you. You know if Carl calls for an accounting, it won't turn out in your favor."

He smirked. "Oh, it'll turn out in my favor. If the sale goes to auction, my buyer will just outbid you, but I think we'd both rather it didn't come to that. I came here to ask what it'll take for you to walk away. Tell Carl you don't want Beachcrest."

Chiara reached out and grasped Auburn's hand, warm and strong and a reminder that she wasn't in this thing alone. She didn't dare give her sister a grateful look—even that would be weakness—but she squeezed back.

"I'm not walking."

Several of the writers cheered.

A muscle ticked in Trey's jaw. "Give it some thought." He cast

Auburn a dark look. "You're going to lose if this gets hashed out in court. Your best bet is to walk away with something that makes you happy. Tuition for your little sister, maybe. A new wing for Cape House. A downpayment for a house for your brother."

She couldn't keep the shock off her face.

He smirked. "I always do my research. You might want to do the same, and then you'd actually know who you're dealing with."

He turned and walked out. They heard the front door chime again, and the sound of his car engine starting up.

There was silence in his wake.

"*He's* a piece of work," Priya said.

"I'm putting him in my next book," Aria said, fanning herself.

"Hero or villain?" Deja asked.

"Hero. Only in my book he'll have a heart of gold."

"Maybe he does," said the fourth romance writer, Lindsey, a fair-skinned redhead and jewelry fiend. "He offered to help Auburn's family."

They all glared at her.

"Okay, okay," she said, hands up. "It doesn't *seem* likely, I'll admit it."

"He's preying on the soft spot I have for my family," Auburn said. "There's no heart of gold in that; he just sees the gold."

She quickly outlined the situation for them—Carl's heart attack, the meeting in the hospital room, the confrontation in the hallway. The legal realities.

"Is he right?" Deja asked suddenly. "Are you going to lose if it gets hashed out in court?"

Auburn sighed. "Probably."

Deja touched her fingers to her lips and eyed Auburn speculatively. "You should do it."

"Do *what?*" Chiara squealed. "You don't mean she should let him buy her off?"

"No." Deja shook her head. "She should ask for something." She shot a look in Lindsey's direction. "Apart from your impossibly optimistic view of human nature, do you *actually* think there's a chance that guy has a heart of gold?"

"No?" Lindsey hazarded. "But ... anything's possible?"

"Right." Deja's voice was beautiful, musical, like rough handmade paper. "So, what I'm thinking is, your only chance, literally your only chance of success here, is if you can get him to be sympathetic with your point of view. Make him see how much Beachcrest matters to you. Make him fall in love with Beachcrest itself."

Auburn barked a laugh. "Him?"

The women exchanged another round of glances. "It's not the *worst* idea you've ever had," Aria said slowly.

"He wants to get this thing done quickly, or he wouldn't have offered to buy you off tonight." Deja cocked her head. "He's got a deadline, and a lawsuit screws with that. You got that, right?"

"You think?"

"I *know,*" Deja said. "He's freaked out. So give him what he wants. Tell him you'll back off, but *only* if he agrees to spend one week with you at Beachcrest. He has to stay here, eat breakfast here, shadow you, do all the Beachcrest activities you ask him to, and stick around for Beachcrest's 4th of July festivities. He should appreciate the full value of the asset he's proposing to sell. And then, if that doesn't convince him and he still thinks the sale is the right thing to do, you step away."

"Wouldn't it be better for her to just ask for money?" Priya said. "That's at least a sure thing. This is pure gamble."

Deja shook her head. "Money guarantees she loses Beachcrest. This way—well, she at least has a chance.

"I—I don't think it's a good idea." Auburn's stomach knotted tight at the thought of Trey Xavier following her around for a week. She cast a quick glance in Chiara's direction, and found her sister eyeing her with sympathy—and open curiosity. A look that said, plainly: *Do you not think it's a good idea because you don't think it'll work? Or because you're afraid of yourself?*

Auburn bit her lip.

"I think Deja's onto something," Chiara said gently. "And Auburn—you won't be alone. We'll all help you figure out how to make this place irresistible to him."

"That's right," Deja said, nodding. "We've all fallen in love with Beachcrest, right, ladies?" She collected a round of nods from her friends. "And we're all experts at getting hard men to fall in love."

Auburn couldn't imagine Trey Xavier, hard man extraordinaire, falling in love with anything. Least of all an inn at the beach. But on the other hand, she'd seen how much fire his eyes could bank. He wasn't entirely cold, not by a long shot.

Something moved in her chest at the thought.

Chiara was watching her again.

I'm not afraid of him, she silently broadcast back at her sister. *Or myself.*

Chiara's eyebrow rose, just a flicker—a challenge. *Prove it.*

"Okay," she said. "Deja's right. It's not much, but it's a chance."

It was a tiny chance. The slimmest of chances. A chance that would require her to spend the next week with Trey Xavier.

She should *hate* that idea. She *did* hate that idea.

Which didn't explain the swirl of excitement in the pit of her stomach.

10

"She's late," Trey said, consulting his watch.

"It's two minutes after," his grandfather said mildly, from his hospital bed.

"She called the meeting. She should be here."

His grandfather chuckled. "I don't think she plays by your rules."

As if he'd conjured her, the door swung open and Auburn walked in. She'd shed her usual athletic wear and wore a pencil skirt, a silky looking blouse, and heels. All restraint except for that insane hair. She looked like a librarian who'd stuck her finger in a socket, and—why the fuck was that hot?

God*damn*, it was impossible not to be thrown off course by her. Yesterday evening, at Beachcrest, he'd felt completely off kilter. The words that had come out of his mouth, his body language—they'd all conveyed the ice calm he expected from himself. But inside, he was churning—with frustration and the need to do something to tame her.

"Mr. Xavier," she said.

It was the first time she'd called him that, and crap. He liked it.

"Ms. Campbell."

Her eyes swept to his, and he saw the flare of pupil. There was that, at least. He wasn't the only animal in the room. The combativeness of the situation—or *something*—was affecting them both. The thrill of a fight. Things had come too easily to him for too long. She was just a challenge. And it must be the same for her, too. No way running an inn provided the kind of thrill she clearly craved.

Damn it, he needed to hold tight to his resolve. Whatever had prompted her to call this meeting, it was Auburn's Last Stand. So ... he needed to keep his focus. Not think about what thrill she might crave.

"I have a deal for you."

Startled, he nearly let his surprise show in his eyes, but recovered himself. "*You* have a deal for *me*."

Her lips curved at that. Which wasn't the response he wanted. "I do. I know you don't want a legal battle, because if you didn't care how long this took, you wouldn't have shown up last night and tried to buy me off."

He'd underestimated her. He'd shown his hand, and either she or her friends had seen through his play. "I just like to keep things simple. And money keeps things simple. I pay you, you go away, this all stops."

Carl made an irritated noise from the bed. Jesus, why had he agreed to meet here? This was hard enough without an audience.

"I *can* make this all go away," Auburn said. "But I have a price."

Ah. So he'd been right about that. Thank God.

"July 8—that's when you need this deal signed, right?"

"Around then," he lied.

He saw her lips curve in a smile, and realized she knew. She knew what the time pressure meant, to him and to her. God damn it. He'd really fucking underestimated her.

"Give me till then to convince you that you should sell Beachcrest to me."

He raised his eyebrows. "Why would I want to do that?"

"Because if I can't convince you, I'll walk away without a legal battle and let you make the sale."

It was too easy. There was a catch.

"But—"

Here it came.

"—it's on my terms until then."

From her pocket, she produced a sheet of paper and held it out towards him. He took it.

"'This is an agreement entered into by Trey Xavier, henceforth XAVIER, and Carl Philburn, henceforth PHILBURN.' Who wrote this?"

"I did," Auburn said.

"Did a lawyer even look at it?"

"Just read it."

"'XAVIER agrees to be a guest at Beachcrest, arriving June 30, checking out July 8. XAVIER agrees to attend every breakfast and every afternoon tea.' Afternoon *tea*? *Of course* you have afternoon tea."

"Beware the power of afternoon tea," Carl said. "You're out of your depth, my son."

Trey rolled his eyes.

"'XAVIER agrees to participate in the following activities: one beach bike ride, the Tierney Bay July street dance, one Beachcrest-sponsored campfire with hotdog roast and marshmallows, the 4th of July parade viewed from in front of Beachcrest, the second annual Beachcrest-Cape House 4th of July barbecue, the 4th of July fireworks viewed from Tierney Bay Beach, and one beach hike,

time and place to be determined. XAVIER agrees to participate to
the extent dictated by Auburn Campbell (henceforth CAMPBELL)
and to be reasonably polite to the other people involved.'"

He raised his eyes at that. "I'm always 'reasonably polite.'"

"I beg to differ," Auburn said.

"We can agree to disagree."

"'If XAVIER fails to carry out his part of this agreement,
PHILBURN will sell Beachcrest to CAMPBELL for a going-
concern value set by a mutually agreed-upon appraiser.'"

Jesus. "This is your big play? I'm going to go on a *bike ride*? To
a *parade*? You think *this* is going to change my mind about
anything? Look—" He thrust the paper back at her. "You know
what a bike ride is to me? An Expresso Fitness S3R Novo in a
climate-controlled gym with a personal trainer standing by. And
a parade? That's something that happens when the WNBA team
I own wins the championship." He omitted the fact that he'd had
to sell his WNBA team—the point still stood. "And the only fireworks I have time for are the ones I give a woman in bed. So if
you think a few breakfasts and *teas* and a bike ride and a parade
is going to change anything, you are barking up the wrong
fucking tree, sweetheart."

Carl had coughed midway through his speech—at the fireworks comment—but Auburn hadn't even flinched.

"If it won't change your mind anyway," she said, sweetly,
"why not just sign the agreement?"

"Because it's a waste of my time!"

"Not as much of a waste as a lawsuit."

"Look, darlin'. I know you think I'm just some kind of rich
asshole—"

The expression on her face told him he'd picked *exactly* the
right phrase.

"—but I'm *not* just doing this to piss you off. The development my friend is building? It's a retirement community. A beau-

tiful, luxurious retirement community. The perfect place for my grandfather to live out the rest of his days in peace and contentment."

It was his trump card, and thank the *Lord*, he could see on her face that he'd gotten through to her. All her certainty had vanished. She looked—confused. She bit her lip, and *oh,* God, he wished she wouldn't do that. It made his mouth go dry.

"I don't *want* that," Carl said.

Auburn turned to face him. He was sitting up in bed, arms crossed, stubbornness written across his face.

"*Beachcrest* is the perfect place for me to live out the rest of my days in peace and contentment. I don't want some prison cell for dying rich assholes. You can build it, Trey, but I won't live there. Not while I can hold a pen and sign my own name."

Now Auburn wasn't even attempting to hide her smile. "You heard the man," she told Trey. "He doesn't want it. So all of this has been for nothing anyway. Let's just cut to the chase, and you can sell Beachcrest to me."

Trey shook his head and addressed his grandfather. "You'll change your mind when you see it. Huge hurricane glass windows—140-degree ocean view in all the units." He felt an unusual twinge of desperation. Why were his family members so opposed to being in clean, beautiful living quarters? Why were they all so determined to resist his attempts to keep them safe and happy?

"I'm not selling it to you," he told Auburn. "I'll change his mind."

"Ha!" Carl said. "You will *not.*"

Auburn pursed her lips. "I might though," she said slowly.

He and his grandfather both froze.

"Carl. If Trey takes this deal with me, the one to give Beachcrest a real chance, you have to agree you won't fight him on the sale. And that you'll live in the new place."

Carl looked from Trey to Auburn and back again. And something like a smile spread over his veiny old man face. "I see what you just did there."

She was clever. Quick. Savvy. Trey had to grant her that. She'd—

Well, she'd outmaneuvered him.

Except for one thing.

There was *no* way she was going to convince him to fall in love with Beachcrest, no matter how much time he spent with her.

Apparently, his grandfather didn't feel the same way because he snorted. "Hell, yes, I agree." He turned toward Auburn. "Make it so."

She laid the "agreement" on the side table and scribbled something, then showed him what she'd added. "'If XAVIER carries out the terms of this agreement, PHILBURN agrees to yield to Trey's wishes in the matter of the sale of Beachcrest.'"

She handed the pen to Trey.

One week. One week of attending events while being 'reasonably polite.' He could do that in his sleep. And if he gave up the next seven days of his life, he could get this deal signed, save Home Base and a hundred and fifty jobs, sell the *shit* out of his company, and hang onto the wealth that would guarantee his sister's, nephews', and grandfather's safety and well-being. It was a no-brainer.

He scrawled his name, then watched as Carl did the same. His grandfather beamed at his protege.

"You've got this, girl. In the bag."

Then Carl turned back toward Trey. "And you? You have *no* effing idea who you're dealing with."

Trey's gaze met Auburn's, and she smiled, a wicked, knowing quirk of lips. Her gaze held level with his, all challenge and confidence. He felt that look, all the way down to where his dick was growing heavy.

All at once, he wasn't nearly as certain as he'd been when he'd signed his name.

Looking at Auburn, her generous curves barely contained by the restrained lines of her businesswear, her hair like its own creature, he had to admit to himself that it was possible Carl was right.

11

Trey Xavier was wearing a *suit* to breakfast.

Of course he was. She hadn't put dressing like a normal person in the agreement, so he was taking advantage of whatever loophole he could to show her he was still in control ... of *something*.

It irritated her. Made her itchy and combative. But it also had another effect on her, one she was trying hard to ignore.

She *liked* it. Not just how good he looked in the suit, but the power it highlighted. The unyielding strength.

As furious as she was with him, she still couldn't help *reacting* to him.

The only fireworks I have time for are the ones I give a woman in bed.

It was just a stupid line.

But her body had believed it, a hundred percent.

Trey was fiddling with his phone. Like, hadn't looked up from it once, despite the easy flow of conversation all around him. Apparently, he was too important for them.

The rest of the guests had, of course, noticed the misfit in their midst, and were eyeing him like a cat in a dog park.

Everyone else was in some variation of beachwear—bathing suits and coverups, shorts and Ts, capris and Ts—or in the fishermen's cases, coveralls and tanks. One of the fishermen gave Trey a thorough once over, while the other glared daggers at both of them.

Auburn bit her lip to hide a smile.

She sidled up to him. "Put your phone away, Xavier."

"You didn't specify that in the deal. You said I had to come to breakfast, not that I had to *participate in* breakfast."

She couldn't detect even a note of teasing. Was it possible he was serious? Yes, given what she knew of him, it was. He was going to split every hair in their agreement and drive her nuts. Maybe he even thought he'd get her to back down that way.

"You agreed that you'd do my activities the way I wanted them done, and that you'd be polite to the other people present. It's rude to be on your phone at the table."

He looked like he wanted to argue, but after a moment he shrugged and tucked the phone away. "I thought you wanted me to like Beachcrest. Making me put my phone away when I'm trying to do important business isn't going to accomplish your goal. And—speaking of doing business, you might want to give some thought to the comfort of your business guests—which is just about everyone these days. The room you've got me in is not well set up. The desk's too small, there aren't enough outlets or charging stations, and the Wi-Fi drops constantly."

"Noted."

She didn't show her anxiety, but getting Trey to slip out of business mode and into vacation mode was starting to feel like an insurmountable task. You could lead a horse to water, but you couldn't make it drink ... you could lead a grumpy businessman to breakfast ...

But you couldn't make him eat it, apparently. And if he

wouldn't taste her food—she was definitely at a disadvantage. "You haven't touched your plate."

"I ate my eggs."

"And left your biscuit, fruit, and bacon."

"Indeed," he said.

"Is that the diet you're on? Avoid anything that would give you pleasure?"

His eyes met hers, dark and ravenous, and she immediately regretted her words. "I wouldn't say *that*."

Her stomach took a dive. "So what's the deal?" She gestured at his mostly untouched plate.

"I don't eat carbs. Or gluten."

"Of *course* you don't. What about the bacon?"

"Fat. Nitrates."

Deja, Lindsey, and Aria reached across the table and helped themselves to a slice each. "Don't mind if we do," Aria said. "Oh, wow. That is seriously good bacon. Smoky. Crispy."

Auburn caught the hunger as it moved across Trey's face, as quick as a flash of lightning. So he was restrained, but he still wanted the things he deprived himself of. Interesting.

She'd love to see him eat. Like, really eat. And not just because she was a damn good cook and food was the best tool she had to make someone fall in love with Beachcrest. But because, well, it would be satisfying to watch him indulge.

All his appetites, a little voice whispered.

Shut up, she whispered back.

"These *biscuits*," Lindsey said, leaning across the table with hers in hand. "You've got to take a bite. A few carbs won't kill you."

He eyed his biscuit like it might leap up and corrupt him, then picked it up almost gingerly.

"You have to butter it," Auburn said. It hurt her heart to see her biscuits eaten without plenty of hot melting butter and—

preferably—lots of strawberry jam. Although she wasn't going to push her luck on the jam.

He glared at her.

"What? Butter is good for you now. I just read an article about it."

"Food fads," he muttered, but he took a bite.

The look that flashed over his face made Auburn's belly heat. It disappeared as quickly as it had come, but she'd seen it. And she wanted to bring it back, somehow, and keep it there.

"Do you share the biscuit recipe?" Aria asked. "I can never get mine to come out."

"I'm putting together a Beachcrest cookbook," Auburn told her.

Aria clapped. "That's so cool!"

"We're going to give the ebook free to everyone who stays here and sell the paperback online. It should be out by Christmas. If you gave your email address when you booked the reservation you'll automatically get a copy without having to do anything else."

"Oh, my, God, really?" Aria said. "Su-weet. When you're ready to sell the paperback, let us know and we'll pimp you on social media."

"Wow, thank you so much."

Auburn's peripheral vision was sharp, or she might have missed Trey reaching for the biscuit.

She turned in time to catch him in the act of taking another bite, and their eyes met. She raised her eyebrows.

"What?"

She took the biscuit from him, buttered it liberally, and handed it back. She could feel his eyes on her face the whole time.

"If I risk my arteries like this, you have to do something for me."

"That biscuit is its own reward."

"For an early death? You need to look at my plans for the retirement community."

"Then you have to eat bacon the next time I serve it." She met the challenge in his gray gaze, unflinching, and she felt something unspool in the pit of her belly.

"Don't push your luck."

He edged his chair away from the table and got up.

She turned away, but she saw, out of the corner of her eye, when his hand snaked out and snatched the biscuit.

12

W hen Auburn came into the kitchen, he was up to
his elbows in hot soapy water.
"What the hell are you doing?"

"The dishes."

"You don't have to do that. And especially not in your nice clothes."

"I know I don't have to." But his mama hadn't raised him to let someone else do all the cooking and then walk away from the mess. Even if the someone was currently doing everything in her power to make his life difficult.

"It's an inn. You're a guest."

"Actually," he said pointedly, "I'm the owner."

The softness that had come over her at the sight of him doing dishes vanished, and she straightened up. "So this is about asserting control. Of course." She crossed her arms.

It had been, at least a little—but it still galled him to be called out on it. "This is about doing the right thing."

"Right." She rolled her eyes. "At least let me get you an apron."

He raised an eyebrow.

"Your shirt costs, what—?"

"Doesn't matter."

"Matters to *me*," she said. All the warmth had vanished from her voice. Which was for the best. Her soft look when she'd first seen him doing dishes had caused an answering softening somewhere in the center of his chest, which he didn't like. She stepped across the kitchen and rummaged in a drawer.

She was wearing a sundress and an apron of her own. The apron had cupcakes on it, each topped with a cherry. The cupcakes looked a lot like tits, a fact that had distracted him mightily at breakfast. Unfortunately, it hadn't kept him from noticing the way her eyes lingered on his mouth.

She'd just been watching him eat, that was all.

He was craving another one of those buttered biscuits. Holy shit, that thing was lethally good. This was why he avoided carbs. Once you went down that path ...

She emerged from her search of the drawer and handed him a Beachcrest apron with a cartoon picture of a plate of bacon and eggs on the front, watched him with an amused expression while he put it on, and turned away to begin loading one of the industrial dish trays.

He plunged his hands back into the suds and set to work.

Work—that was what he was good at.

"More dish soap?" he asked.

"Under the sink."

He knelt to get it, and— "Shit—you've got a leak."

"Yeah. That's been going on a while. It's slow. Not a big deal."

"You should fix it." He knew himself well enough to know that he wouldn't be able to stop thinking about it until he'd found a toolbox and repaired it himself. It was his greatest strength and biggest weakness as a business owner—a streak of perfectionism he couldn't shake.

She heaved a sigh. "Carl was going to fix it, and then— He'll get to it when he gets back."

"You know, it's that kind of thinking that makes Beachcrest look the way it looks."

"And how exactly is *that?*" Auburn asked, crossing her arms over her chest. His eyes kept being drawn to the gap where her pink lace bra barely managed to restrain the creamy curve of her breast.

"Shabby. Like someone will 'get to it' in a few days or a few weeks."

Pink heated her face, and her eyes flashed. "Look, asshole, we don't have an infinite amount of money! We have to triage. If you cared so much about the upkeep of Beachcrest, you could have showed up at any point and contributed to repairs."

"I tried to give Carl money for upkeep," he said with a shrug. "He wouldn't let me. He didn't want me any more invested than I was."

Her mouth opened. "Oh. I guess that makes sense." She bit her lip. "Sorry I, um, called you an asshole. About that, anyway."

He waved a hand. "I've heard it before."

After a moment, she said, "Shabby, huh? You really hate this place?" She didn't sound angry anymore. Just *curious.*

"I don't hate it. I just—don't see what you see in it. To me, it's just ... plain Jane."

A bemused expression passed over her face. "Which is part of what I love about it. It's comfy. Cozy. Like a good friend. You say shabby, I say comforting. Besides, what's wrong with plain Jane? *I'm* plain Jane."

He raised an eyebrow. It was true she wasn't model beautiful. She wasn't expensively dressed, or buffed and coiffed, smoothed and polished, by trained professionals. She wouldn't stand out in a crowd, except maybe for her hair.

And yet, he'd picked her out from a bar full of women, and

the last few days had done nothing to mute his interest. Those goddamn cherries looked more and more like nipples to him as the morning wore on, and he had to keep shutting down his brain as it trundled off to imagine what hers looked like ...

She tilted her head. "I suppose whatever you and your buddy are planning to build on this lot will be top of the line, state of the art, and definitely not shabby?"

He wrenched his brain back to this zip code and the reality of their situation, where there was no possibility he'd ever see her nipples. "Hang on. I'll go get the plans."

"Don't bother."

"I did eat the biscuit," he reminded her.

"What a hardship," she mocked.

Okay, true, it hadn't been much of a self-sacrifice. Tender, flaky, and buttery—and it had been a long time since he'd indulged himself, so it had tasted like heaven. And the expression on her face—

"What the hell," she said with a sigh. "Show me the plans, Money Bags."

He gave her a look, and she shrugged again. "I just tell it like I see it."

He jogged out to the freestanding guest house where his room was—the mother-in-law apartment, as he liked to think of it—then back to the kitchen with the roll of plans the developer had shared with him. He spread them on the center island.

There were architectural drawings and colored-pencil 3D concept drawings, and she looked them over quietly, without comment. "Clean lines," he said, pointing. "Modern. Everything's green—LEED Silver—"

She looked up at that. "Nice."

"We've clustered the buildings to preserve as much land as possible. These are all windows here, see? Carl would be looking out over the ocean every day for the rest of his life. Even Beachcrest doesn't have views from every room, does it?"

"No," she admitted. "But Carl doesn't *want* to live in your retirement community."

"Sometimes people don't know what they want," he said. "Who wouldn't rather live someplace like this—new construction, every amenity, comfort first—instead of—"

He didn't finish the sentence.

"You know, Beachcrest isn't just a *building*," she said. "It's an experience. That's why I'm making you spend this week with me. So you can see some of the magic firsthand. Stuff happens here. Amazing stuff. Old friends, honeymoons, reunions, wedding anniversaries. People falling in love, falling in love all over again, meeting strangers who change their lives, seeing people they haven't seen in years. People realizing they're not living their best lives and starting over again, people realizing they're living their best lives and haven't been appreciating it and vowing to do better—

"There were these women, high school friends. They'd fallen out after a drunk driving accident; each blamed the other for not stopping what happened that night. They'd been close as sisters before. They ran into each other here, each with their separate families, and at first they pretended not to know each other, but their kids wanted to play together. Kids somehow know how to teach their parents to be better people. And one morning at breakfast, one of the women said, 'I don't hate you, you know. I never hated you. I hated myself.' And they both cried. They've rekindled their friendship. They come sometimes at Christmas, together, the two families."

It was a good story; he had to admit it. Not that it said anything about Beachcrest, the way she thought it did. "They could have run into each other anywhere, couldn't they have? Their kids could have ended up in school together."

She rolled her eyes. "And you think that would have been the same? Kids in school together?"

She looked so disgusted that he figured she was probably done trying to win him over with stories, but then she said, "You know the fishermen?"

He nodded.

"They've been fishing together for a couple weeks every summer—this is their tenth year. They came here as 'just friends,' but when they're here, they're not 'just' anything. Beachcrest is the one place they can be *together*. I don't know why that is, I don't ask. I just know that they feel safe enough here—and Beachcrest did that, you know? And they keep coming and getting stronger, growing more sure of themselves and each other. Then they leave and go back to their own lives. But this is *the* year, I can feel it. They won't go back to their corners again. You'll see. I'd love to host their wedding here, eventually. If there is an eventually for Beachcrest."

She'd gotten animated. The curve of her cheeks had flushed pink, her mouth a lush near-red. She pushed her hair out of her face and leveled that cobalt-blue gaze at him, like she was daring him to contradict her.

Damn it. She wasn't plain Jane at all. She was pretty as fuck.

Wait.

No.

He'd cut this deal with her—this deal with the devil—because it was the clearest, fastest, most expeditious route to what he needed. He couldn't afford to soften toward her, toward Beachcrest—especially not at the behest of his dick. Doing so would be like handing the devil his soul on a silver platter.

He gathered up the plans, not bothering to fold them.

"Thanks for looking," he said, and got the hell out of the kitchen before he couldn't stand the heat anymore.

13

A s soon as the kitchen was clean, Auburn took off for the Cape House Hotel to talk to her older brother. She walked away from Beachcrest and the ocean, up the short sand-strewn road that bore Beachcrest's mailing address, and turned right onto Tierney Bay's main drag. Her path took her past other inns and bed-and-breakfasts, a few up-and-coming restaurants that were tailoring themselves to the increasing number of well-to-do tourists in town, and her favorite coffee shop—she waved through the half-steamed plate glass window at Em, the barista.

Scrappy.

Scrappy!

Fuck him.

And yet for one brilliant second, after she'd told him the story about the fishermen, there had been something in his face. He was listening. He wasn't a block of ice to the core.

Maybe her chances of making him fall in love with Beachcrest were near nil, but they weren't absolute zero.

She couldn't guarantee she could change Trey's mind, but she could make sure she was ready to take action if she did.

And to do that, she needed money.

The closer she got, though, the more she dragged her feet. It wasn't that she was *afraid* to ask Levi for money; it was that she wasn't sure she should be asking him at all.

She had to hike up the hill to Cape House. It was one of the biggest hotels in Tierney Bay—twenty times more rooms than Beachcrest. It also drew a different clientele, one seeking luxury and amenities rather than "cozy comfort," which was nice because it meant that Carl—and by extension she—and Levi weren't really in competition.

She found him in his usual spot—behind his desk in the administrative office. He didn't look up when she came in. He had a spreadsheet open—par for the course—and was tweaking the rows and columns. "Give me a sec," he said.

It wasn't a request. Levi didn't make requests.

She settled herself in his guest chair and prepared to wait.

Levi owned Cape House, and had since their parents died in a boating accident when Auburn was a teenager. For a while, Levi had hired managers to run the hotel, but he'd turned out to be incapable of taking a hands-off approach. Now he worked with two assistant managers who tolerated his control freak tendencies, one with amusement, one with barely suppressed irritation. He was always busy, but he also always had time for his siblings, and Auburn knew if she waited patiently, he would give her his undivided attention.

When he finally looked up, his first words were, "We need more weddings."

Auburn was used to her brother leaping into the heart of a business conversation. "If you want more weddings, you're going to have to start kissing up to Grace." Grace Utrecht was the town's best wedding planner and one of Levi's least favorite people. The feeling was mutual, which hadn't helped Levi book weddings, since Grace's referrals carried a lot of weight.

"So be it," he said grimly. "I didn't put all that money into this place to watch it spiral down the drain because Grace and I butt heads."

Auburn thought "butt heads" was putting it lightly—Levi and Grace's battles were more like the overture to World War III, but she left it alone. "How are things going with the improvements?"

Levi had borrowed against the hotel a couple years ago to upgrade Cape House from "just" a tourist hotel into an event center. The last of the renovations were finishing up now, just in time for the hotel's first big event, which happened to be Chiara's ten-year high school reunion.

Levi sighed. "There've been a few unexpected setbacks," he said. "I made the mistake of going with the cheaper bid on the pool, and I'm paying the price. I thought we'd be on a better footing by now than we are. I had to borrow deeper than I'd meant to. We'll be okay, we are getting bookings finally, but—it's going to take more time than I thought before I can pay off the loans."

"Levi, *no*," Auburn said, alarmed. "You should have said something."

"What would you have done about it?"

"Between us, Chiara and Mason and I could have—"

Even as she said it, she knew how ridiculous it was. None of the siblings had the kind of money Levi would have needed.

It was Levi's turn to grind the word out. "*No*. Chiara's just finished paying off her loans. Mason's saving for a place of his own, and God knows how long *that'll* take him at his current rate. And you—" His eyes softened as he took her in. "You've had a tough enough year without worrying about me. I'd be shocked if you had two nickels to rub together. No offense."

It was nearer to the truth than she'd like to admit, and hit too close to home. "I'm *fine*."

"Well, I'm glad to hear it, but like I said, it was my problem to solve. You've got Carl's illness on top of everything else."

The mention of Carl was the perfect segue into her own request. *Speaking of Carl, speaking of Beachcrest, speaking of money, speaking of my tough year, speaking of what I want, what I need, what I love—*

She opened her mouth.

And closed it again.

"Did you—did you come here to ask me something?" Levi asked, his eyes suddenly sharp on hers.

If she asked Levi for money, he would find a way to give it to her. He'd borrow against the last scrap of equity in the hotel for her; she knew it. Just like he'd left behind his own life to come home to take care of his siblings. He'd given up medical school and his dreams of becoming a doctor to run a business he'd never shown the slightest interest in. And he'd done it all so the family could stay together, in the only home they'd ever known.

Meanwhile, he'd postponed saving for his own future so one day he could pick up where he had left off.

If she asked him for money—even assuming there was any left, which didn't sound likely—he'd give it without hesitation. Even if it destroyed his second chance to chase his own dreams.

There was still Hannah, too. She was sixteen, and—as Trey had sussed out—college loomed for her, another expense on Levi's horizon.

There was no way in hell she would ask Levi for money.

Onwards, then, to the banks.

She shook her head. "I was just in the vicinity and I figured I'd stop in and say 'hi.'"

"You're always welcome," he said. "And you know, there's always a job for you here if—"

"I'm good," she said quickly. "I've got Beachcrest."

She would make sure it stayed true, and she would do it without stealing anything else from Levi's future. That was the least she could do for the brother who had held their family together.

14

"I don't know what you heard, Patrick, but if I needed your money, you'd hear about it from me, not from your client."

Trey froze at the sound of Auburn's voice, clipped and decisive.

He'd come over to the office because his Wi-Fi wasn't working, but before he'd turned the corner into view, he'd heard her. And even though he knew he should retreat before he eavesdropped anymore, he couldn't quite make himself do it.

"Yeah, look. I appreciate your concern, but I've got this Beachcrest situation under control. And I will tell you—*myself*—if that changes and I need anything from you." She listened for a moment. "No. No, that's definitely not necessary. And not a good idea. Patrick, no." She was quiet again, then said, "All right. I appreciate that. Take care."

Trey rounded the corner just as she swiped a finger across her phone to hang up the call and swore under her breath. Her eyes came up to meet his. He should pretend he hadn't heard her ... but his curiosity was killing him.

"Who's Patrick?"

Practical considerations, he told himself. He needed to know where things stood on her end, so he could strategize.

"You heard that?" She frowned.

"I just came to tell you the Wi-Fi's down *again*."

She gave him a look.

"I'm providing useful guest feedback," he clarified. "I need to send some long emails, and the phone's not cutting it for me. But back to my question: Who's Patrick?"

He was justified in asking, right? It concerned him if this guy related to his business deal. If she was asking for money from someone, that affected—

Well, he couldn't exactly say how it affected him, but it felt important.

She sighed, heavily. "My ex. Apparently he heard about the Beachcrest sale from his client, who's your—chief operating officer?"

Doug. He wondered what Doug had told this Patrick guy. Hopefully not the whole story. The last thing he wanted was for rumor of his dire situation to creep back to Auburn ... and Carl ... and Brynn. No, he wanted to clean this up long before that had a chance to happen.

Then the substance of what Auburn had said finally penetrated his overtaxed brain. "Your ex offered you *money*?"

She frowned at him. "You don't care how I get the money, do you?"

Actually, he didn't, and if he had his way, she wouldn't need to get it, because this whole farce would play itself out, he'd earn Carl's agreement, and he would sell Beachcrest to Royal Life Group, the luxury retirement company.

Which didn't explain why he wanted desperately to know what the hell her ex was doing sticking his nose into this.

Because the guy could have financial clout or legal power. Because Trey couldn't deal with any additional swerve in this process right now. That was why. Not because Auburn was no longer wearing the tit cupcake apron and all her curves were on display and it was taking most of his self-control not to ogle her. Not to think about the body underneath that pretty sundress.

"Do you have a good relationship with him?"

He hadn't meant to ask that.

Her lips tightened. "No, I wouldn't say that. And—you know what? This is really none of your business. It has nothing to do with you or our agreement."

"Actually, it does. Why does this guy care if you need money anyway?"

She gave him a hard, dark look, and for a moment he was sure she wasn't going to answer. And really, he couldn't blame her. If *he* wasn't even sure why he was asking her, he couldn't expect her to respond. Then she slumped over the desk, resting her head on her arms. "Because he wants me back. And he's richer than God, and he thinks if he can convince me that I need his money, it'll give him a way in." She spoke into her forearm, but the words were distinct enough, even through the cloud of her curls.

"Will it?"

Not his business. Not his question to ask. She'd have every right to tell him to go to hell.

She sat up, and her dress slipped to reveal the edge of pink lace against the satin of her fair skin. His mouth went dry. "Not in a million years."

He recognized the slippery emotion in his chest as relief. Which—

What. The. Fuck.

And no. Just no.

"Wait a minute," he said, his brain catching up with what she'd said. "Richer than God? Patrick who?"

"Patrick Moriarty."

"You were with *him*?" he demanded.

"You know him?"

"Not well. But our paths have crossed. We move in some of the same circles."

"Yeah. I figured, from the fact that he's chummy with your COO."

"He's also a prick."

That made her laugh. She had a good laugh. Real. From the belly.

"I mean, way worse than I am." Patrick was Trey's least favorite kind of man, the kind who kissed ass to people's faces and screwed them behind their backs. Who came on like a hero to women, and treated them like shit in private. Totally inexcusable in Trey's book. And that asshole had had his hands on Auburn. Had touched her all over.

Not that he should have an opinion about that.

She gave him a wry smile. "Yeah. He turned out to be not such a prize, though he treated me like I was one. A prize he owned."

Some things that hadn't made sense to him before were starting to make more sense. "That's why you turned me down at Bob's. Because you think I'm like him." And he hadn't really given her any reason to think otherwise, had he?

"I turned you down because I don't do casual sex and you came on like an arrogant prick."

"Oh, is that all?"

She laughed again. It felt good to make her laugh. He could turn making Auburn laugh into his own personal crusade.

Which—shit, no. He couldn't. He was going to tear down her inn and break her heart, which was the exact fucking opposite of making her laugh.

"Where's the router?" he asked gruffly. "I'll see what I can do about getting the Wi-Fi back up for you. Can't ink this deal if I can't send email."

The humor fled her eyes and lips, and he regretted it—but he had to be realistic about this situation. About *himself*.

"Over here," she said.

He caught her glancing at him a moment later, though. Searching his face, as if trying to catch a glimpse of something he'd kept hidden from her.

Smart girl.

15

S he needed to stress bake.

After her visit with her brother, she'd sat down with Chiara and set up a Bootstrapper page, then trudged into town to visit all four banks and credit unions. Two had said no outright.

It wasn't that they were unfriendly. They were eager to do business with her, in the form of a twenty percent-down mortgage, which—they explained hastily—was already generous—hotel loans usually had down payments of twenty to fifty percent. But since they knew her family, and her brother had a proven track record, and she herself had so much hotel experience ... *if* she could raise the money for a twenty percent down payment some other way, they'd be overjoyed to loan her the rest.

The third and fourth lenders ...

Keegan Horan, an old friend of her father's, and Diane Cooper, who'd worked with Levi on the Cape House loans, had both said they'd see what they could do. They'd asked her to send them all her financial information and they'd assess the possibility of extending her a low- or no-down-payment loan.

They'd promised to get her an answer, one way or the other, by Friday, the day after the July 4th holiday. Keegan had been his usual gruff but reasonable self, and Diane had been gentle and sweet, but Auburn wouldn't exactly characterize either of them as brimming with optimism. More like—not wanting to burst her tiny little bubble.

Still—it was *something*.

Of course, before the money could matter, she still had to win over Trey. And he obviously didn't want to be won—every time she thought she'd begun to see a glimmer of his sympathetic side, he hid it away beneath that icy exterior. Could you make someone fall in love with something if he was determined not to? The romance writers clearly thought so, and they'd assured her they knew their stuff. Auburn wasn't so sure. Trey didn't seem like a guy who'd just ... slip-slide his way into anything.

And there was always the chance that he'd just flat out lie, even if she *did* win his sympathies. Say she hadn't.

Except the one thing she sensed from Trey was that he was honest. To the point of bluntness, in fact. She couldn't imagine him *lying*.

But she really didn't know him at all, did she? She'd thought Patrick was a decent guy, too, until it had been impossible not to see the truth.

Oh, bloody hell, this was such a mess.

Making cookie dough always calmed her down and cleared her head.

Auburn made loads of dough at a time, then froze it so she could bake a batch of assorted cookies fresh each afternoon— chocolate chip, ginger molasses, peanut butter, snickerdoodle. Prepping new batches of dough couldn't help but restore her equanimity.

Only, when she made her way back to the kitchen, there was

a man on her floor with his head under her sink.

Trey.

Wearing jeans and a soft gray t-shirt. The first time she'd seen him in anything other than businesswear.

The t-shirt had ridden up and the jeans had ridden down—just a little—showing a narrow band of golden ridged stomach and just the very top edge of the place where his skin turned white and his hip muscle dove—er, south.

That little bit of pale, bare skin did something weird to her insides. It was like a visual reminder that Trey had an underbelly, a vulnerable side. That he was a mere mortal like the rest of them.

She was afraid that if she startled him, he'd hit his head on something, so she held very still and watched, probably for longer than was appropriate. The jeans were well-worn and clung to his thighs, and when he wiggled to adjust his position, all the muscles she could see bunched and flexed and—

Her mouth was dry, which seemed to be because all the liquid in her body had pooled, like hot gold, between her legs.

She turned, tiptoed out of the kitchen and stood outside it contemplating her next move. She tried very hard *not* to think about the thigh muscles she'd seen under his jeans. Or any of the other contours his jeans had made, hugging his body...

She needed a clear head to do this. She could not, could *not* afford to be attracted to Trey Xavier. If she lost her head, she had no doubt he would rampage over her like ... well, like a construction vehicle clearing ground for a new development.

She re-entered the kitchen, making as much noise as humanly possible. It worked. He slid himself out from under the sink. His t-shirt rode up even further, but he yanked it down when he saw her. "Oh. Hey."

"Hey," she said. "What are you doing under my sink?"

"I had to fix that leak."

His phrasing struck her oddly. "You *had* to?"

For a moment she thought he wasn't going to answer. Then he sighed and sat up. His eyes were troubled, the sky over the Pacific before a storm.

"I hate anything that's broken or ugly. I have a—I guess you'd call it a compulsion—to fix it. Comes from growing up in a shithole."

She could tell from the way his gaze jumped away from hers that he'd said more than he'd meant to. And that made something squeeze in her chest—maybe just hope for his humanity?

Okay, so he'd grown up in *a shithole*. Huh. She guessed she could see it. Beachcrest was successful but not minting cash or anything, and there were all Carl's investment troubles, and Brynn had alluded to the fact that she and Trey hadn't grown up with money. That meant Trey was self-made at some point in his history.

It cast things in a different light. The way he talked down about Beachcrest, scorned its shabbiness. His obvious need to gild the world.

"Let me show you what I'm doing, so you can do it yourself next time," Trey said.

She realized he was asking her to get down on the floor with him and look under the sink. And that—

That would put them very close together in a horizontal position.

"I don't bite," he said wryly.

"I'm not scared of you," she said bullishly. She got down on the floor and slid in beside him. Lying down made her feel shockingly vulnerable. Which made *no* sense, because he was on the floor, too. But she felt like—like she'd just exposed her *own* pale white underbelly to him.

Worse, she could feel the heat coming off him, all along the length of his body. If she turned her head ...

Don't turn your head.

"See this? This is the valve handle, and this is the packing nut. So I just wrapped a rag around the nut, gripped it with these —" He produced pliers— "and turned it about one-eighth of a turn. It compresses the rubber, and usually that's enough to stop the leak. In this case it was. But if it happens again and you can't fix it this way, you'll need to disassemble the valve. Or find someone who can."

"Well, it won't really matter if Beachcrest is gone, will it?"

The words popped out before she could stop them. She hadn't meant to let her bitterness show. In order to beat him at his game, she needed to have ice in her veins, like he did. She couldn't be leaking feelings out all over the place.

"No," he said, quietly. "No, I guess it won't."

She'd expected a note of gloating in his voice, but there was none there. Which was somehow more unsettling.

And then she made the mistake of turning her head, at the same time he did, and their faces were—almost touching. She could feel his breath move over her lips.

She hastily slid away from him, feeling cold all along the side of her body and hating herself for noticing. She stood, and he stood next to her. There was a long moment of almost painful awkwardness, and she burst out with the first thing that popped into her head.

"Where'd you learn about plumbing?"

"I flipped houses for a while."

"Was that your first business?"

"No. My first business was leaf raking and lawn mowing. Age twelve. My dad sucked with the house upkeep. It bugged me."

"Because you hate things that are ugly and broken."

"Yeah."

He looked away from her, like his compulsion to make things better and more beautiful was something to be ashamed of.

"Then what? After the leaf raking and lawn mowing?"

"That grew into a full-on landscaping company. After that, house painting. Through high school."

"Then?"

"Contracting. Then the house flipping. Then that turned into real estate development. And then real estate technology. When I was flipping, I'd wished I had an app that would make flipping and other sales more efficient. So I found a guy to develop one for me and turned it into a business."

"A very successful business, word has it."

He dipped his head. The modesty of the gesture made her feel like she'd read him all wrong. He wasn't an arrogant asshole. So why had he come off so much that way in Bob's? Was the way she saw him tinged by the deep grudge she still bore against Patrick?

"That's—that's really impressive."

His eyes raked her face, like he was trying to figure out if she was putting him on.

"I mean it," she said.

"Well. Thanks. It was just what I had to do."

"How so?"

Something in his face tightened, and she thought he wasn't going to answer. Then he took a breath and spoke again.

"Things weren't great at home."

She wanted to ask him more, but she knew she'd pushed him far enough. Something dark and shuttered in his face told her that part of the conversation was over.

"Do you miss it? Fixing things? Building things? Instead of—"

"Moving money?" he asked, amused.

"Well, yeah."

He opened his mouth to answer, and then paused. Seemed to consider her question.

Abruptly, he reached out and touched her arm near the shoulder.

For a moment their eyes held, and held, and held. She heard every tiny sound in the kitchen. The purr of the fridge, the odd rattle of the ice maker, the tick of the old-fashioned analog clock Carl loved.

Then his hand dropped away, leaving a trail of warmth where it had touched. "You had something on your shirt from the floor. A dust bunny." He held it out.

Oh, for the love of God, it was just a stupid dust bunny. She was totally losing her head, her body blooming like a June rose at the unexpected touch.

She needed to pull herself together and get her mind fully back on what mattered. Saving Beachcrest.

"Oh, look at that," she said sarcastically. "A little bit of shabby stuck to me."

She took the dust bunny from him and tossed it in the trash, then got the broom and swept along the edge of the sink. When she was done, she took out the mixer.

"I'm making cookies. For afternoon tea. Which is on your schedule."

"What kind?"

"Molasses ginger, snickerdoodles, oatmeal raisin, and choco- late chip. Hot and fresh from the oven."

"I like chocolate chip best." There was a hint of lust on his face, the same as when he'd bitten into the buttered biscuit, and it was enough to make her heartbeat kick up.

It was just because she liked feeding people. That was all.

"Nuts or no nuts?"

"I'll make some of each."

"Good. Because chocolate chip cookies shouldn't have nuts. It ruins the gooeyness."

She couldn't help it, she smiled. "Did you just say

'gooeyness?'"

He shook his head. "Must have been someone else."

She startled herself—and him too—by laughing. "So you'll be there."

"I'll be there. I agreed to follow the schedule, didn't I? I don't break my word."

I was right, she thought, and then, *shut up, you're so naive.*

For a moment she doubted the entire wisdom of the plan. Because saving Beachcrest was *not* worth losing her self-respect again. Not by a long shot.

But no one was asking her to sacrifice her self-respect. She could take a deep breath, tamp down the unruly scraps of attraction, and Get. This. Thing. Done. Wherever they went, including afternoon tea this afternoon, there would also be other people. The romance writers, the fishermen. Reinforcements. Buffers. It would be relatively safe.

"Will there be milk, to go with the cookies? I'm not exactly a dainty tea drinker."

And, after all, he was the one showing weakness. He was the one who'd slid under her kitchen sink, who'd picked a dust bunny off her shirt, who'd used the word "gooey," who'd admitted that chocolate chip was his favorite.

She should be thrilled by the fact that he was showing himself. Showing a soft, almost *playful* side. Because it was a sign that Beachcrest's magic was working on him.

But it felt like the most dangerous thing of all.

She knew. The danger was inside her. It was her weakness. For his body, honed by expensive gym equipment, his power, stoked by years of ambition, and his money. The same weakness that had left her at Patrick's mercy.

"Ice cold," she said.

It was an answer to his question about the milk, but also a reminder to herself.

16

A uburn moved around the room as Trey watched. Chatting. Laughing, with a toss of her curls. Carrying trays of cookies from one guest to the next, offering them to the writers, the fishermen, the family.

She giggled at something her front desk clerk said to her, then threw an arm around the other woman's shoulders. She looked up and her eye caught his. Damn it. He looked away.

He had tried, several times, to stop watching her, but every time he thought he'd tamed the impulse, he found his eyes on her again.

Something bad was happening.

When they'd lain under the kitchen sink earlier, he'd been unable to think about anything except her closeness. They'd turned their heads at the same time, and he'd heard the hitch of her breathing and thought about what it would feel like to lick into the wet heat of her mouth.

It would fuck everything up. Right now, this was all very straightforward. He just needed to march through this schedule of hers, remain sufficiently indifferent, and *win*.

The fact that he'd been able to completely forget his mission for at least three inhalations and exhalations, long enough to fall into a rhapsody involving her tongue, was a bad, bad sign.

Luckily, she'd jumped away before he'd really had to test himself. Of course she had. Because he'd been an asshole to her. Because he was still being an asshole to her, going through the motions of what she'd asked him to do while still planning to screw her in the end, and not in the way he'd imagined doing when he'd seen her at Bob's.

Except there was the way she'd looked at him when he'd touched her shoulder—

It wasn't the way you looked at someone you hated.

Which only made things worse, of course.

He should probably do something completely assholic so she would hate him again. One of them should have their head on straight.

"Here," she said.

She had a glass in her hand. Filled with milk. He took it from her, and it was ice cold against his palm.

"You remembered."

"Of course!" she said. "That's my job."

She handed him a chocolate chip cookie, still warm, and watched him closely as he took a bite.

He couldn't hide how damn good, tender and flavorful and chocolatey, that bite was, and her pupils flared, setting up an answering curl of heat in his groin.

She'd be like that during sex, he thought suddenly. She'd watch him like that, and her pupils would widen with sympathetic pleasure as he drove into her.

In bed, their combativeness would be smoking hot. She'd demand what she needed and meet him stroke for stroke and crest for crest. They'd go up in flames.

His cookie had gotten suddenly tasteless, like it wasn't

possible for his body to enjoy both the pleasure of Auburn's baked goods and the fantasy of her getting off on his arousal.

She was still watching him, and there was something on her face, an echo of his non-cookie thoughts.

If he hadn't had both his hands full, he would have—

What? What would he have done?

Nothing, because acting on that particular impulse would be suicidally stupid.

"It's delicious," he said, instead. "You can make a cookie."

She grinned knowingly. "I'm glad you like it."

"Auburn." It was the mother from the family of four. "You're out of snickerdoodles. Are there more?"

"There's another tray over there," Auburn said. She bit her lip as she turned to walk away from him, and he had to resist the urge to stop her with a hand on her arm.

The fishermen came down, grabbed a ginger molasses cookie each, and sat on the couch together. Not quite touching, but their non-cookie hands were interlaced. Trey didn't think he had a romantic bone left in his body, but Auburn's story must have gotten under his skin because he felt a small curling sympathy in his chest for them. He tried to imagine having made it that far in life without ever admitting to yourself what you really needed. What it would feel like to have those needs met. The sense of liberation would be overwhelming.

At least, that's what he would imagine if he had a heart. Good thing he didn't. It would be such a liability in this situation.

He looked up from them and found Auburn watching him. He gave her a slight nod, like the tip of a hat. *I see, now.* A smile spread over her face. He could *feel* that smile, like it was moving in his bloodstream.

"Well, well, well." Deja, the ringleader of the romance writers, had appeared at his side. Her eyes moved from his face to Auburn's and back again.

"Don't," he found himself saying.

"Don't what?" she asked.

"Don't do whatever you romance writers do."

"What *we romance writers do*," Deja said primly, but not unkindly, "is believe that love conquers all."

Across the room, the father and mother were talking to each other and laughing, her head thrown back, his hand reaching out to push strands of hair off her face.

Perversely, it made Trey think of something that had happened when he was ten. His father and mother, talking in tense tones after they thought he was in bed.

I kill myself to keep this family solvent. I worked for that money. And you gambled it away.

She didn't mean literally. Trey's father wasn't the casino or cards kind of gambler. He loved *schemes*. And he believed in them. He was sure he'd find one that would change everything for them.

What had struck Trey that night was not his mother's words to his father. It was that his mother was crying as she spoke. *His father had made his mother cry.*

He'd vowed at that moment, he would *never* be like his father. Weak, impulsive, so unwilling to work hard that he'd rather grasp at a thread that could pull everything down like a house of cards. He'd never be the kind of man who would make a woman suffer because of what he couldn't give her.

"I'm happy for you if you can believe that," he told Deja, "but in my experience, love doesn't conquer anything. Unless by 'conquer' you mean 'destroy.'"

"Do you really think that?"

It wasn't Deja's voice, but Auburn's, at his shoulder. Her gaze searched his face, avid and curious. It made him feel like she could see right through him.

And the worst part was, he had no idea what she would see if she could.

He *owned* the fucking inn. It was his to do whatever he wanted with. In a few days, it wouldn't matter what she thought of him or what she saw when she looked into his eyes.

So why, for the first time in a lifetime of doing business, did he feel like he was operating at a disadvantage?

Like *he* was weak and impulsive and on the verge of doing something he'd regret?

He set his half-drunk glass of milk down on the coffee table. His second cookie, too.

"I've got some emails I have to answer," he said. "You can check teatime off the list."

Deja was still looking at him. Hard.

"You go do that, then," she said. "We'll all still be here, enjoying each other's company, believing what we believe. Devouring what we wish to devour. Speaking of which, if you're not going to eat that other cookie, hand it over. Someone needs to teach you to quit wasting food."

17

A uburn pounded on the door to the guest house.

"What?"

"You missed breakfast, and you're supposed to be biking on the beach with me right now. Technically, you're in violation of our agreement."

She was sure his absence had something to do with the unusually personal conversation she'd overheard between Trey and Deja. The one that had ended with him declaring that love destroyed things. Auburn had tried to get Deja to tell her what had led to Trey's dark utterance, but Deja had just shrugged. "All I said was that romance writers believed that love conquered all. And he went off."

Auburn suspected that there was more to Deja's story than she'd told, but she hadn't been able to pry any more information out of her.

She also hadn't been able to stop thinking about Trey since last night. She'd lain in bed and wondered at the vehemence in his voice and what had brought it about. She had all these pieces of him, like a puzzle, but they didn't quite fit together. Something was missing. And she wanted to understand what it was.

Love doesn't conquer anything. Unless by 'conquer' you mean 'destroy.'

Those were big words.

"I have a work emergency I need to take care of." Trey's voice came from a distance.

"Can you come to the door so I can stop shouting at you through it?"

She waited long enough that she wasn't sure he would, and then he did, opening it barely enough for them to converse through the gap, like he was trying to keep something out. Her. And he wouldn't quite look at her, either. "Look. I have things I need to take care of. I need to take a rain check."

"We have a deal. You promised me a week."

"Yeah, well, I'm unpromising."

She closed her eyes and took a deep breath, trying not to lose her temper with him. She opened them and said, "If you don't want to do the deal, that's fine, but I'm not going to just give up on Beachcrest. If you can't go through with this, we can do it the hard way, with a partition action. And maybe I'll lose, but maybe I won't. Carl has a good claim on sweat equity in the property. He might convince a court to sell it to me. You and I both know if you didn't think that was a possibility, you wouldn't have signed that contract with me."

"That contract would never hold up legally."

"That's not the point, Trey. If you don't honor your deal with me, this whole thing is going to be out of both of our hands. And I don't think either of us wants that."

She was pleased to hear her voice come out strong and sure —far surer than she felt.

He paced away from the door, to the other side of the room. Back again. His expression was dark. He reached up, pressed a hand against the wall over his head. Leaned in and sighed heavily. "Okay," he said, finally. "Give me a minute."

She eyed him. "You can't go dressed like that."

He was wearing brown linen dress slacks and a cream button-down, both gorgeous specimens that clung to his muscular body like a second skin. She knew the fabric would be soft to the touch, and the urge to reach out and test that theory made her fingers itch.

Quit it, she admonished herself. *This is enough of a mess without you bringing sex into it.*

"I'll change into jeans."

His expression was bland, almost blank, the same cool, impersonal gaze he'd leveled at her in Carl's hospital room, in the dining room at Beachcrest when he'd tried to buy her off, and when she'd presented him with her deal. Like she was just a minor irritation. Gone was any hint of the warmth he'd shown her yesterday, or the teasing.

Something had sent him back into his shell.

Well, fuck it, she'd drawn him out once, and she'd do it again.

"You can't wear pants for beach biking," she said levelly. "You'll roast. You need shorts or swim trunks, and sandals would be good."

"I don't have those."

"You're at the beach with no shorts or swim trunks."

"I'm only nominally *at the beach*."

"Have you even been down on the beach at all yet?"

He shook his head.

She sighed. "I'll ask Levi if you can borrow some of his beach clothes."

He shook his head. "No way. I'm not wearing some other guy's swim trunks or sweaty sandals."

She looked him over. Just thinking about riding a bike in

pants made her uncomfortable—let alone with the sun blazing down on them. "We're going shopping, then."

"Where?" His eyebrows drew together, suspicious.

"Let me worry about that."

"In town? Because there aren't any real stores in town."

She rolled her eyes. "Deal with it."

"You're going to make me go to one of those tourist traps, aren't you?"

She raised her eyebrows. "You'd hate that, huh?"

He nodded.

"Then, yes, definitely."

The corner of his mouth lifted, almost imperceptibly. Was that an actual smile? Yes. It was barely detectable, but she didn't need to be able to see it to confirm it, because she could feel it in her chest. She'd made Trey Xavier smile.

He could retreat into his turtle shell, but she'd lure him out again. For Beachcrest.

And for her. Because the mystery of him reached out to something inside her. Because she'd seen those hints of warmth —of softness—and goddammit, she wanted to pull him apart like a warm chocolate croissant and lick out the "gooeyness" inside.

Not *literally*, of course. There could be no licking.

She tried to imagine what he'd have to say if she shared that metaphor with him and had to cough back a laugh.

"What?" he demanded.

"Just—finish up and get your butt out here. We have *real* work to do."

18

"No," he said, hanging back on the sidewalk as she stepped forward, toward a shop called Sea Stuff. "I can't shop in there."

The two large storefront windows brimmed with beach clichés—pastel colored women's coverups, pillows that said "Everything's Better At The Beach," a frisbee with a sand dollar on it, a rainbow kite, a folding shovel with an octopus decal. An assortment of cheap jewelry bearing sea star charms and exhortations to "Love" or "Breathe."

"You *can,* and you are."

"No. It's a tourist trap. No, worse: It's the tourist trap that all tourist traps were made in the image of." He actually found himself stepping back, a dramatic retreat, and realized: He was doing it to try to make her laugh. Damn it. He had to quit that.

After his conversation with Deja yesterday afternoon at tea, he'd nearly bailed out of the whole deal. Before he *did* something he'd regret. For example, kiss her.

Although he knew that wouldn't be the worst thing he could do. The worst thing would be to *like* her. Generally speaking, Trey went out of his way not to have feelings—even mild ones—

for people he did business with—particularly if those people's interests were not aligned with his.

If he liked Auburn Campbell, it would be that much harder to do what he knew he had to do.

Deja had seen him looking at Auburn and had recognized what he'd been trying to deny since that first night in Bob's Tavern, that despite the mess on the table between him and Auburn, he couldn't look away. Because she was pretty, yes, sexy, hell yes, spunky, feisty, spirited, yes, yes, and God, yes. But the thing he liked most about her was how she saw the upside of everything. Goodness in everyone. Beauty in the things that were shabby, broken, or ugly. Fun in little bits of nothing. Which made no sense, because he had no patience with that kind of sentimentality. None.

And in this case, he could absolutely not afford it.

"You don't need designer clothes to bike on the beach," she said, and before he could argue, she swung the door open and marched in.

Mouth open, he followed her.

She led him toward the back of the shop, where she began pulling things off racks and piling them into his arms. "Go. Try those on."

"Are you always this bossy?"

She made a face at him. "Only when a rich, out-of-town asshole shows up and threatens to tear down my inn."

He squelched a smile. "Not your inn. *My* inn."

She scowled and gave him a little shove toward the dressing room. "Shut up and get naked."

His eyes found hers, but her expression gave nothing away, which made it ten thousand times more annoying that his body had reacted so instantly, a hum of blood southward. Or was it their back-and-forth a moment earlier that had done it? The stakes were way too high for any of this to be a game, and yet, she made him feel like it was.

Another thing he didn't want to like about her.

Inside the fitting room, he examined what she'd picked out for him. A long-sleeved SPF surf shirt that said Tierney Bay and a cheap pair of Hawaiian print board shorts. Canvas-strap flip flops. Jesus. Talk about ruining someone's life. But he obediently put them on and checked himself out in the mirror. He didn't look anything like himself. His hair was even standing on end from the clothing change. He looked—

Well, he looked like a beach rat. A surfer dude, minus the bleached long hair. And the tan. But even that—he'd somehow picked up some color the last couple of days, maybe when he'd taken his laptop out on the porch yesterday afternoon.

He tried to think whether there was anyone else on earth that he'd ever allowed to dictate his wardrobe choices. Dress him.

No. Definitely not. He'd even quit letting his mother shop for him before he was twelve.

And yet he'd given Auburn the privilege, and he didn't even resent it all that much.

He stepped out. She was standing there, leaning against a column. She was wearing a floaty white shirt that was mostly sheer. He could see through it to her bright red lace bra and her creamy curves. He could see the outline of her navel in the sweet curve of her belly. His eyes traced that soft slope down under the waistband of her skirt.

His hands wanted to follow the path his eyes had taken, dip into her—probably red lace—panties, and wrestle control from her. Preferably by making her lose it completely.

"Well, look at you," she said. "You look almost like you know how to relax and cut loose."

Her gaze traveled unabashedly over his bare feet, up his bare calves—leaving a wake of heat—and up. It traversed his abdomen and fanned out over the span of his shoulders. He could feel the approving perusal like a touch. And his body, Judas that it was, leapt accordingly.

Her attention snagged on the action in the unforgiving board shorts and came up to meet his eyes, sharp and interested. The heat and tension built between them until he could feel the blood moving everywhere. High in his cheeks, fast in his chest, hard and hot where it counted.

She wants what I want.

"Auburn—"

"Finding everything okay?" a voice asked from behind him.

"Yes—" he said, his attention flicking away from Auburn for just a split second, but it was long enough. When he looked back, her face was carefully blank again. Wiped of everything that had been there a moment before.

"Get changed," she said, not looking at him. "And then we can fight over who's going to pay for your new outfit."

Even as flustered as he felt, that made him smile.

19

A uburn unlocked the shed and they dragged the recumbent bikes and a pair of helmets out and hauled them down to the beach.

It was the perfect early summer day—warmer than average for the beginning of July, with the sun sparkling off the water and turning it the same blue as the sky. The sand was burnished white-gold all the way down to the tide line. They tugged the bikes to the packed wet sand near the water.

"So? What do I do?"

"You sit. And put your feet on the pedals, and your hands on the handlebars." She indicated the two short poles sticking out on either side of the seat. "These are how you steer."

He eyed them suspiciously, and she grinned.

He tried to sit in the bike's slung canvas seat and promptly tipped over and deposited himself in the sand.

He laughed.

Like, actually *laughed*.

Rich and deep and genuinely amused. And oh, fuck, she liked it way, way too much. She'd thought she was a sucker for the all-business version of Trey Xavier, but it was nothing compared to how much she liked the rumpled beach-ready version.

"This is a plot to take me down a notch, huh?" he asked, turning his smile on her and taking years off her life.

He hauled his ass out of the sand, brushed himself off, gave her a bemused look, and tried again, managing it better the second time. He pedaled around, gingerly at first, then gaining both speed and confidence.

"See that?" She indicated the monolith in the distance. "Breaker Rock. That's where we're headed."

They set out side by side. It had been a while since she'd taken the bikes out, and she'd forgotten how much work it was. But fun too. He was faster than she was—which made perfect sense because his body was a finely tuned machine. His new trunks had ridden up a little, and she had a full-on view of his thighs, bulging with muscle, dusted with dark gold curls. Nghngh.

She was still unsettled by their exchange in Sea Stuff. It had taken almost the whole walk back from town for the pulse between her legs to quiet. For her nipples to soften so they weren't so sensitive against the lacy cup of her bra. And for her brain to start working again. Slowly, but surely.

Nothing had *happened.* But she wasn't sure what would have transpired if the salesclerk hadn't shown up at that exact moment. There had been something in the way Trey had said her name, to say nothing of the obvious evidence of his interest …

And it hadn't been one-sided. She'd felt the tension drawing tight between them as they'd tussled verbally, and she'd stepped over the line first. Even if she'd regretted her words—"shut up and get naked"—a second after they'd popped out.

She had to be more careful. She wasn't one of those people who could get physical with someone and not have it mess with her emotions, and she wasn't one of those people who could ignore her emotions and make antiseptic, logical decisions.

Ergo, there could be nothing physical between her and Trey. She could never close the circuit, connect those two sparking wires, feel his power jump the gap into her body.

Nope.

He struck out ahead of her, then came back, once, then twice, the third time riding around her in a circle. "I'm your satellite!" he called.

His playfulness tugged in her chest. This—*this* was exactly what her plan depended on. But more than that, it satisfied the part of her that loved Beachcrest. The part that loved cooking for people, taking care of them, and watching them bloom and relax under the vastness of the ocean sky.

She hadn't fully realized it, but she'd *wanted* this. To see him shed the seriousness. Trey playful was something else.

Abruptly she stopped the bike. "This is beach magic."

"What? What are you talking about?"

She threw her arms out. "How big it feels. How airy. Like it can swallow everything. You could take everything in the world seriously, but not out here."

She thought he'd fight her—if only on principle—but he just looked thoughtful.

"I did this once before."

"Rode beach bikes?" she asked.

"Yeah. When I was visiting Beachcrest as a kid."

Her mouth opened. But of *course* he'd been here as a kid. Why hadn't she assumed he had? "You stayed at Beachcrest?"

"A few times, a few summers, when my mom was still alive."

"Did you like it?"

He nodded. He'd closed his eyes—remembering, she thought.

She stayed quiet, although she was desperate to ask questions. She knew if she pried, he'd clam up.

Then he opened his eyes, and there was a whole world in them.

"I got to leave everything behind. All the bullshit. And I hero-worshipped Carl then. My own dad was—"

He stopped.

"Your dad was—" she prompted.

His gaze flicked, startled, to hers. "You really want to know?"

It felt like the safe answer was probably no. But the real answer was yes, and she couldn't bring herself, with the sea and sky all around them, wide open, to be less than honest.

"Yeah. I really want to know."

He looked out at the ocean. Seemed to weigh a whole world of possibilities. Then took a deep breath.

"He was a drunk, and not a nice one. He never hit, but he yelled. And he flailed—broke shit, ruined shit. Couldn't hold a job. Then he'd get into these risky schemes to try to make the money he couldn't make nine-to-five. But my granddad ... Carl ... ran his own business. He bought and sold other real estate; he had this aura of being in control. He talked about what it took to run a business. You had to be gutsy and confident and cool under pressure. You had to be able to negotiate for prices and deals. You had to be careful about cash flow and you had to know the difference between earnings and profits. Hell, he taught me double-entry bookkeeping.

"So we'd come out here with both my parents and my dad would sit on the beach and drink beer and my mom would nap in the room. Brynn would read. And from the time I was little, I'd follow Carl around everywhere. He helped me set up my first business."

"He told me that," she said. "A lemonade stand?"

He nodded. "There were a few small ones like that—lemonade, dog-walking, leaf-raking, and then I started my yard care business—and I told you the rest. But Carl was always there to help. I didn't see him a lot, but I always knew I could call him, if I had questions."

"What happened?"

He looked at her blankly.

"With Carl," she prompted. "You guys were so close back then. And he taught you all this stuff. You said you hero-worshipped him. But not anymore, huh?"

"I grew up," Trey said, and turned away from her.

She thought he was done talking. She almost started pedaling again. But then he turned back.

"I don't know if you knew this, but when he almost lost Beachcrest, that wasn't the first time his investments had blown up in his face. It happened when I was a kid, too. I didn't realize it till I was a teenager, but despite all his big talk about what it meant to be a businessman, and all the money he moved around, there was never any to spare. When I confronted him about it—years after the first time he lost big—he swore he'd learned to be more conservative. And I think for years he was ... but then he almost lost the inn."

There was frustration on his face, but also—hurt.

She drew a deep breath. "He disappointed you."

Trey closed his eyes. "I thought he was so different from my dad, but he *wasn't*. He was just like him."

"You're being way too hard on him," she said. "He's a good man."

Anger flashed in his eyes. "You don't know anything about it."

Abruptly, he started again, cycling way out ahead of her toward Breaker Rock. She followed, not quite ready to catch up. There were so many questions swirling in her mind. She knew there was still more to the puzzle. She could feel it.

They rode out until they were directly across from the rock, then came to a stop next to each other, facing the sea. The rock was hundreds of feet tall, jutting straight up out of the ocean, covered with seaweed and barnacles, circled by gulls and dotted with puffins. They stopped and Auburn offered Trey a drink from her water bottle and a chocolate chip cookie. His face was calm again, any trace of anger gone.

He took a big bite. "You know that scene in the Matrix where he eats the chocolate chip cookie?"

She smiled. "Yeah."

"Is this like that? You're the oracle? And you foretell my future?" The wind ruffled his hair and blew his t-shirt against his chest.

She shook her head. "It's not *that* kind of magic," she said, echoing her words of the other day.

He took another bite and looked out to the horizon. It was blue as far as he could see. Good weather ahead.

He drew a deep breath.

"When we came here, Brynn and I would play on the beach. Even though at home she barely gave me the time of day because she was off with her friends. But here we'd play for hours. And I'd —"

He ducked his head.

"I remember thinking the beach could soak everything up. My dad's crap and my mom's unhappiness. All Brynn's trouble-making. And my own—whatever. Everything."

When he looked up at her again, his eyes were full of emotion. More than she'd ever seen there. She understood. For whatever reason—maybe even *he* didn't understand why—he was giving her this.

"Beach magic," she murmured.

He nodded. "What about you?"

"What about me?"

"Your parents. Your childhood."

"My childhood *was* the beach," she said. "My parents owned Cape House. I thought everyone lived like I did, able to run out onto the beach any time they wanted. It was a big shock to me in college, the first time I met someone who'd never seen the ocean. I didn't even want to believe that was a thing. It was like meeting someone who'd never seen the sun."

"I never thought of that. What it would be like to grow up with that being your every day."

"It was pretty idyllic. But my parents died when I was sixteen."

He froze, the way people so often did when she dropped that bomb. It was part of why she so rarely brought it up. Because you couldn't just let it slide into a conversation and not have that conversation be instantly transformed.

"They were killed in a boating accident."

"I'm sorry," he said.

"Thanks. Levi—my oldest brother—inherited the hotel. And us. Chiara and I were old enough to basically take care of ourselves, but he had to try to be a dad to Mason—who was a tough teenager—and Hannah, who was six. She was an oops baby when we were all already almost out of elementary school. So, yeah. Everything changed then."

He watched her with an indecipherable look on his face.

"It was a long time ago," she said. Sometimes you had to say that to get people to stop looking at you like you were a piece of glass that was about to shatter. But Trey's expression, the intensity of his gaze, didn't soften.

The sun disappeared for an instant behind a cloud that hadn't existed a minute ago. She shivered, suddenly, the sweat now drying on her skin.

"You're freezing."

"I'm fine," she insisted.

His gaze fell to her arms, which were covered all over with goosebumps, the downy hairs standing on end.

With a single, smooth move, he reached behind him and tugged his long-sleeved t-shirt over his head and handed it her. "Here. Put this on."

She was cold enough to reach for it, which was a mistake. When she had it in her hands, she could feel its warmth and softness and she could smell him on it, musky and overwhelmingly male. She sat there, shirt in hands, teetering on the recumbent bike seat, teetering in all sorts of ways. The wind had made his hair all windswept, and he looked like a beach rat instead of a billionaire—in the best possible way. His skin was golden, his pecs taut with muscle and dusted with darker-gold hair. A trail of that hair arrowed down and slipped beneath his waistband.

Her gaze snapped back to his face.

He was watching her, and she couldn't read the expression in his eyes.

"We should head back," she said abruptly, pushing the shirt into his hands. "I'll warm up as soon as we're moving again."

She turned the bike—almost dumping herself in the sand—and pedaled back toward Beachcrest, leaving him in the dust this time.

20

"I still don't understand why you think bringing me to a street dance is going to help your case," Trey said. "I don't like crowds, parties, food carts, or loud music. And I don't dance."

"You also don't like biscuits, bacon, afternoon tea, tourist traps, beach clothes, bike rides, or *me*."

"I *don't* like tourist traps," he said. "Or you," he added, mostly because he wanted to see what would happen.

"You're no prize yourself, Xavier," she said, right back at him. It edged up his heart rate. Because he didn't mean it, so maybe she didn't mean it either.

Not that it would do him any good. God *damn* it, he needed to stop wanting things that were not going to happen. Like whatever hadn't happened in the dressing room this morning. And that other thing, that hadn't happened on the beach. The world was full of things he was not going to do to Auburn Campbell, kisses he would not give her, places on her body he would never put his tongue, and surfaces he would never lay her down on. It was getting harder and harder—pun very much intended—to remember what was on the line. His business, his financial future, his reputation, and a hundred and fifty or so jobs.

"Okay," he said. "Some of those things are okay. Parties, food carts, and music are negotiable. But I *don't* dance."

"I would have been shocked to discover that you did," she said dryly.

They were waiting in line for pulled pork sandwiches, surrounded by the hubbub of people enjoying themselves. And he could tell Auburn was enjoying herself, too. She was wearing another little sundress—it just brushed the midpoint of the back of her thighs, which were paler than the rest of her body. He wanted to lick a line from the back of her knee to—

"I'll make you a deal," Auburn said. They were nearing the front of the line. "You get the mac and cheese and cornbread, I'll get the corn on the cob and cole slaw. And then we can share. You don't want to miss any of them. I swear."

He squinted at her. "There are a lot of carbs in that meal."

"I know," she said, grinning. "I'm super excited about them."

When they reached the front of the line, he dutifully ordered what she'd instructed. He pulled out his wallet and waved hers away. "It's on me," he said dryly, which made her laugh, remembering the first night at Bob's.

"Actually, it *is,*" she said, and she took a napkin and swiped at the barbeque sauce that he'd managed to get on his shirt.

He eyed the stain. "Damn."

"Amateur. Follow me."

She led him to the rickety folding tables covered with plastic checkered tablecloths, and they set down their cardboard trays. It was six p.m., but the sun still beat down. In Tierney Bay, as in most of the Pacific Northwest, 4th of July weekend was when summer started—and two bottles of cold beer sweated between them.

"Carbs," he said, pointing to the beers.

"Yup." She pulled her hat brim down and pushed her sunglasses up her nose. There were a few pale freckles on it. He'd swear they'd come out today during the bike ride. Also, the skin under the freckles—and across her cheeks—was pink.

He reached out and brushed a finger across the sunburn, and she flinched.

"Sorry," he said quickly, although he wasn't, because now he knew what her skin felt like—softer than his favorite silk boxers. "You just—you got some sun. Looks like it might hurt later. Didn't anyone ever tell you to wear sunscreen on the beach?"

She smiled. "Might have heard that a time or two. Following orders isn't exactly my strong suit."

He smirked. "No. And that's an understatement." He bit into his sandwich, tender pork slathered in Carolina barbecue sauce and topped with cole slaw. The perfect combo, the cool mayo soothing the slight spicy heat of the sauce, the bun tender and eggy. He'd just plain old forgotten how good food that was bad for you could be. "Oh my *God*."

"Still not your scene?"

He rolled his eyes at her and dug into the mac and cheese. Holy crap. Soft and creamy and just the perfect amount of breadcrumbs—

"Hey! Leave some of that for me!" She stabbed her fork in and pushed his away. They fork-fenced over the remaining elbow noodles.

He yielded the last bite and she slid it voluptuously off her fork. He didn't think she was doing it on purpose, it was just the way she was about food, all in. That said, he was feeling a little jealous of that fork, which was getting the full-on treatment.

"How old were you when you started working for Carl?" he asked her, to stop himself from thinking about how her mouth would feel on him.

"Fifteen," she said. "I worked for him every summer in high

school and college, and then took a permanent job with him after college. Until I went to New York."

She stopped.

"Patrick."

"Yeah."

"So—you were in New York—how long?"

"Two years."

"That's a long time. As long as I was married."

"You were *married*?"

"Yeah. Couple of years. She left. Said I was a workaholic."

That wasn't *exactly* what she'd said, but it captured the spirit well enough. Abruptly, he got up. "Let's walk."

They tossed their garbage and strolled together up and down the street for a bit, scoping the scene.

The street dance shut down Tierney Bay's main drag all the way from one end of the retail zone to the other. Booths selling all kinds of food and drink—as well as arts and crafts—lined the sides. Kids blew bubbles, drew with chalk, and messed with silly string. If you walked half a block in either direction the music changed as you passed each small makeshift bandstand—blue-grass, Zydeco, country, garage rock.

It was pretty fucking charming, actually.

What happened if she succeeded? If she made him fall in love with Beachcrest?

He wasn't going to think about that.

The band whose zone they'd just stepped into was playing "Seven Nights to Rock."

"I *love* rockabilly," Auburn said, and started dancing.

And oh, *fuck*, she looked good. The shimmy of her breasts, the wiggle of her hips. He wanted to put his hands on all of her at once. Which was—

Well, there was one permissible reason to do so.

He pulled her into a dance frame—ignoring her startled

look—and edged her into a passable West coast swing, dredging the moves up from the depths of his soul.

"You *do* dance! You were holding out on me!" she said as they swiveled in and out and he spun her away into a turn, caught her at the apogee, and tugged her back.

She felt amazing in his arms, her smaller hand in his, his face tucked down near her ear, his lips against the soft satin of her hair. She smelled unbelievably good. Strawberry shampoo and a vanilla-and-cinnamon scent that he was pretty sure was *her*.

"I said I *don't* dance, not that I can't." He slid her down his leg, which made her giggle. When he drew her back up and turned her toward him—their faces so close he could smell the bright malt of beer on her breath, he said, "I learned for my wedding, but this is the first time it's ever been my choice."

Startled, she looked up at him. Her eyes were bright, her lips parted—soft and red. She licked them and he heard his breath huff out of him, but somehow, some-freaking-how, he managed not to kiss her. It felt like the world would probably end if he did, and also if he didn't. So for now he'd take what he had, which was the softness of her curves in his arms.

"Trey—" She bit her lip, and his cock, just an inch from her thigh, twitched.

"Just—don't," he said. "If either of us talks, we'll probably say something we'll regret, don't you think? And I'm enjoying this way too much for that."

She opened her mouth again, then closed it. For a long moment, he was sure she was going to shut them down—and she'd be more than right to. Then she took a breath. "Do that thing again. With the—" She gestured as best she could with him still holding her hand.

He let his own held breath out in a rush. "This one?"

He swung her out so they looked at each other down the

length of both arms. Her smile was gone, and she was looking at him like—

Like she didn't hate him.

Like she *really* didn't fucking hate him.

He hadn't thought he liked dancing. He hadn't been bullshitting her. But apparently he just hadn't tried it with the right person. Because this? This slow fucking burn? It was better than most actual *sex* he'd had.

Which didn't stop him from wishing he'd met Auburn under any other circumstances. And it sure as fuck didn't stop him from wanting more.

———

21

It was the perfect night for a beach fire—clear and warm, with a little breeze.

She'd built the fire an hour ago and tended it ever since, and her guests had gradually come down to join her, sitting on log benches to form a cozy circle around the burning driftwood.

The fire had formed coals now, and she brought out the hotdogs and passed around the long metal forks with wooden handles.

Normally, there was no happier place for her than sitting by a beach fire, but tonight, she could barely sit still. She was so full of feelings, she couldn't even tease them apart and name them.

She'd driven Carl home from the hospital earlier today—Brynn had been tied up with kid activities—and was thrilled to see that he'd seemed almost like his old self. He'd been so glad to see Beachcrest that his eyes had glistened with tears, which had made her weepy, too.

He'd wanted an update, of course, on the *situation.*

Well? he'd demanded. *Did he come around yet?*

No, not yet, but...

But you're doing a beach fire tonight, right? And tomorrow is the 4th. And no one does the 4th better than Beachcrest. He has *to admit that.*

No one does the 4th better than Beachcrest, she said, because she was sure about that. And pretty much nothing else.

The fact that she was helping Carl get resettled at Beachcrest had forced her to cancel the beach walk she'd had on the schedule for Trey. Which was maybe okay? Because she was still really confused about what had happened last night at the street dance. The dancing part.

If either of us talks, we'll probably say something we'll regret, don't you think? And I'm enjoying this way too much for that.

She'd felt such a rush at that—as if he'd confessed way more than just that he liked dancing with her. And the way he'd looked at her a moment later, when she said, *Do that thing again.* Like she'd just asked for something dirty and perfect, something he'd been wanting to do for days. Her whole body had gone hot. Liquid.

He was sitting a short distance away. He'd arrived on the beach with his sister and the two boys in tow. He was wearing some of the clothes she'd picked out for him yesterday. And something had softened in his walk too. It wasn't so much of a stride. More like a lope, now. Relaxed. He looked like a man on vacation.

He'd accepted a beer and a hot dog—speared it with a male wince on a long-handled barbecue fork—and thrust it into the heat of the coals. He'd taken a second fork and was fire-roasting two more dogs for his nephews. And he hadn't even given Auburn a lecture on the dangers of processed meat or fillers. Or the carbs and gluten in beer.

He was smiling and laughing, chatting with the fishermen about how he used to go fly fishing with his dad in Montana when he was a little kid. He finished up his hot dog, tugged it off the fork with a white-bread bun—no griping about the white carbs, either—and took a huge bite.

"Damn," he said to no one in particular. "I forgot how good these are."

Part of her was elated. She'd done *exactly* what she'd set out to do. She was maybe even a little ahead of schedule, since he was already in an expansive mood and they hadn't even broken out the marshmallows.

She'd turned a businessman into a beach rat in seventy-two hours.

And unless she was very much mistaken, she had at least a fighting chance at convincing Trey that Beachcrest belonged right where it was—and right as it was.

Then why was she all churned up inside? She was accomplishing just what she wanted.

And yet she wanted something else, too. For his attention to leave the hot dogs and his nephews and the fishermen and settle on her. For him to stand up from the log where he sat, cross to where she was, and sit too close for casual conversation. Close enough that the heat of his body would outshine the heat of the fire.

She wanted him to linger at the fire after the other guests left and—

And more.

All she had to do to get Beachcrest was to stay the course. Pretend that dancing and toasting marshmallows with him was enough.

But it wasn't.

And that scared the living shit out of her.

Her face was flaming hot, and the smoke had changed direction and was blowing in her face. She stood up and moved into the shadows.

Chiara, who'd also come down for the roast, joined her.

"What'd you *do* to him?" she asked her sister. "It's like he was under the curse of a wicked witch and you kissed him and saved him."

"Er," Auburn said. "There hasn't been any kissing yet."

"Yet?" Chiara was all wide-open eyes and mouth.

"There isn't going to be any kissing. At all."

"You said, 'yet.' I heard you."

"It was a slip of the tongue."

"It sounds like tongues might start slipping any moment."

"That would be a very, very bad idea."

"And yet—*yet*—I'm getting the distinct feeling you haven't dismissed it as a possibility."

"I'm trying to do a business deal here. I can't imagine this could *possibly* help."

"You're trying to get him to fall in love," Chiara said. "Kissing always helps with that."

"With *Beachcrest*," Auburn said. "I'm trying to get him to fall in love with *Beachcrest*."

"I hate to break it to you sis, but you *are* Beachcrest." Chiara's face was all mischief, but before Auburn could protest, they were joined by Brynn; Auburn introduced the two women.

"I need to get myself a s'more before they run out of marshmallows," Chiara said. "Anyone else?"

"I wouldn't turn one down if you arranged for one to be made for me," Auburn admitted.

"I'm good," Brynn said, waving a hand. "Hey," she said to Auburn, as Chiara stepped back toward the fire. "I just wanted to say that I'm on your side. About the inn. I'm opposed to this whole retirement development thing. I think Trey should let Beachcrest stay, and Carl should come live with me. But Trey's against that."

"Against Carl moving in with you?"

"He's got a bug up his ass about stuff like that. He doesn't even want me living where I am, let alone Carl moving in there. He tried to buy me a new place. I told him where he could shove *that*."

"He tried to buy you a new place?" Auburn could feel her mouth fall open.

"Yeah. He hates my house. And to be fair, it's a little bit of a shit heap at the moment, but it's my shit heap, you know? I earned it with my own damn money after I got myself back on my own damn feet after I made my own stupid-ass mistakes."

That made Auburn smile. "Funnily enough, I do know."

Brynn smiled back at her. "Yeah, well, tough to get my big, bad brother to grok that. He needs to save all of us with his bajillions of dollars."

They both turned and looked at Trey, who at the moment was spearing a marshmallow on a fork and looking a lot more like the small boys surrounding him than like a rich man with a savior complex.

"He's in such a good mood today," Brynn said. "I was shocked when he asked if the boys and I wanted to come to the campfire with him. I was like, who are you and what did you do with my brother? I think it's the effect of the beach. He always loved the beach when we were little."

"He was telling me about it. You guys coming here. Playing on the beach together. He said it was a happy time."

"It was. But then after our mom died and Carl was so angry with dad—" Brynn closed her mouth abruptly. "I should shut up. Trey wouldn't appreciate me flapping like this about him."

"Brynn!" Trey came toward them. "Can you Google something for me? Tyler wants to know how marshmallows got invented. He also wants to know what marshmallows are made of, and I can't say I have an answer for that, either. Actually, maybe I don't want to know, given how many I've eaten."

"Google it yourself, doofus," Brynn said.

"I left my phone in my room."

Brynn's mouth fell open. Auburn was pretty sure her own was a mirror image.

"You left your *phone* in your *room*?"

"Yeah. Can you Google it for me?"

"Sure," Brynn said. "And while I'm at it, I'm Googling 'symptoms of alien abduction,' too."

22

"Don't let me eat another marshmallow. No matter how much I beg." Auburn closed the bag with a rubber band and tossed it into the wheelbarrow.

He liked the idea of her begging. A lot.

There was a smudge of marshmallow just above her upper lip, and he hadn't been able to stop thinking about it for the last five minutes or so.

"Was it my imagination? Or were you having a good time tonight?" she teased.

They were the last two people down by the fire. Brynn and the boys had left after a few rounds of s'mores. The romance writers had headed back to the B&B a few minutes ago, leaving Trey and Auburn on their own.

"If I admit I had fun, will you use it against me in the quest to win Beachcrest?"

"Hell, yes. I'll take any advantage I can."

"Then no. It was a total drag. I hated roasting hot dogs. It gives me *the willies*—pun intended—to spear phallic fake meat on a long-handled fork. No one likes their meat flame broiled. And s'mores suck, you know what I'm saying? All that toasty marshmallow and *gooey*ness."

She gave him a shove and he fell backward onto the sand.

"Okay," he admitted, climbing back onto his driftwood seat. "It was fun. I like the fishermen. Once you get a few beers into those guys and get them talking—the story about fishing with Barack Obama was great. Do you think that's true?"

Auburn shrugged. "No reason to doubt."

"Rick said something about how they'd be back next year, and you should have seen Dewann's face. I think you might be right. That they're not going back to their separate corners."

Auburn smiled. "Told you. Beachcrest magic will get them in the end."

He frowned. "So, what, how does it work? Everyone falls in love at Beachcrest?"

"Everyone gets what they *need* at Beachcrest. Love, redemption, friendship, clarity, whatever."

As she spoke, there was a glow on her face that wasn't just the firelight. Her hair was a riot in the light breeze, curls everywhere. Her eyes bright. And that goddamn splotch of marshmallow. He made himself look away, because otherwise he was going to do something he'd regret.

"Brynn said you don't want Carl living with her."

"I don't."

"What's that about?"

"She has it tough enough, taking care of the boys, without throwing a senior citizen who's recovering from a heart attack into the mix. Not to mention that her house is in way worse shape than Beachcrest."

"But if she wants to—"

"People think they know what they want, but they don't. She doesn't have the resources to take care of herself and Carl. She's so stubborn. She'll take on more than she can handle."

"She told me you tried to buy her a house."

"Jesus, Brynn," Trey said to the sky in exasperation. "Can't a man have some secrets?"

Auburn smiled. "That was nice of you. To try to take care of her that way."

"Yeah, well, she didn't think so."

"I understand that, too. She wants to do it for herself." She was quiet for a moment, looking out to where just a few streaks of lighter sky still shone out of the dark. "Trey?"

"Yeah?"

"What happened between Carl and your dad?"

He felt like he'd been smacked in the chest. "What did Brynn tell you?"

"Just that after your mom died, Carl was angry."

He knew that if he shut her down now, she wouldn't push. He couldn't say how he knew that, but he knew.

So he wasn't sure what made him step into it. Right into the heart of it. Call it beach magic. Or Auburn magic. Because increasingly, he was beginning to think that that's what it was about. What she called beach magic or Beachcrest magic was really Auburn herself, the way she saw. The way she listened. The way she cared. Magic happened around her, all right, but not because of something outside her. Because of what was inside her.

"I told you my dad drank. Couldn't hold down a job. Got into crazy schemes."

She nodded, eyes huge.

"My mom made up for it. Worked two and sometimes three jobs to compensate."

The old pain had seized him around the chest, tightening like a vise. It was tough to breathe. Like how it must have been for his mother.

"She got sick at one of the factory jobs. They didn't have adequate ventilation for the particulates, and she ended up with all kinds of breathing problems. They thought it was asthma, but it turned out to be lung cancer. Stage four when they caught it. It was so fast. Less than a month, if you can believe it."

"Oh. Oh, *God,* Trey."

"Working like that killed her," he said quietly. "*He* killed her."

She reached out a hand and took his. Without stopping to think about whether he'd regret it, he turned his hand in hers so they were holding hands for real. Ran his thumb over her smooth skin.

"Is that why you do what you do? Make money so you can keep everyone you love safe in gilded cages?" Auburn paused, pushed her hair out of her eyes, drawing his gaze back to her face. "You don't want to be anything like your father?"

"I'm nothing like my father," he said.

It came out harsher than he'd intended—but not as forceful as it felt in his gut.

"No," she said, thoughtfully. "I don't imagine you are."

Her eyes held his until he couldn't stand the intensity and looked away. "Gilded cages, huh?" The characterization hurt—but he recognized the truth in it, too.

"I'm sorry. That was harsh. I know you're just trying to do what you think is best. For Brynn. For Carl."

"No," he said quietly. "I think you're probably right. And I probably did it to Karina, my ex-wife, too. She left me a year ago. After I canceled the first vacation we'd booked in two years. Because a deal fell through and I needed to fix it."

He wasn't expecting Auburn to be sympathetic. He knew it had been an asshole move. But that deal had been a big next step for him, and he hadn't been able to walk away from it.

He thought Karina had understood how important it was to him. He thought she understood that it would practically guarantee that nothing could touch them again financially. He thought she understood that literally everything he'd done from the moment he'd met her had been *for* her. Every hour he'd worked, every dollar he'd made. To keep her safe, make her happy, ensure she never suffered or needed anything.

Auburn's eyes were soft. "I'm sorry," she said, and it made his chest hurt like hell.

"I just wanted to make things good for her," he said. "But I guess it's like you said. I kept her in a gilded cage."

She kept her gaze on him. It was too dark to see the blue of her eyes, but he could see their intensity and their clarity. The curve of her cheek, the softness of her mouth. And that tiny splotch of sticky-sweet.

Maybe he just needed to defuse the intensity with which she was watching him. Or maybe it was because it was a small imperfection on a perfect face. But for whatever reason, he couldn't stand it any longer. "You have some marshmallow. Here." He pointed.

She tried to lick it away, the tip of her tongue just short of where it needed to be. He reached out and put a hand behind her head, his fingers weaving into her hair.

He heard her breath catch—and felt his own echo it.

He gave her a beat to protest, but she didn't.

He drew her close, leaned in, and licked the marshmallow from her lip, nibbling to make sure he got all of it. He pulled back and looked at her. Her breath came fast. He couldn't see the color in her face, but he could see the lust-drunkenness in her eyes.

Come to me. Come to me. Come on, Auburn. You said Beachcrest always gives people what they need.

I need you.

He wondered if it worked even if you didn't say the words out loud.

He was still wondering when she slid her hand into his hair and pulled him in.

23

The breeze ruffled her hair, and his mouth landed hot on hers, and the combination decked her.

Her nipples, already hard in the cool air, knotted so tight they almost hurt, and she could feel all those sensations —the nibbling at her lip, the tightening of her nipples— arrowing down to her clit and her core.

She kissed him back more or less out of self-preservation, because it was more sensation than she could stand and it had to go somewhere.

He was a good kisser. He gave her slick heat that echoed itself between her legs. He showed her he was in charge, which made her even wetter. He nibbled and thrust and bit and teased, and she whimpered.

"You like that?" He pulled back just enough to ask it.

"Yeah," she whispered.

He kissed her again. Their mouths felt made to be together. She was empty and hungry and craving and wanted him to fill her up. Instead, he made her emptier by finding the bare skin at the bottom of her shirt and sliding his hand up so slowly that she wanted to scream. By the time he cupped her breast through her lace bra, she was pushing herself into his palm. Which made him groan, low and rough. He kissed her again. Little kisses. Bigger kisses that invited her to open for him. His tongue, sliding against hers. Exploring her. Owning her.

"God, Auburn, you have no idea how much I've been wanting to do this."

"Me too," she whispered.

"Tell me you like it."

All she could do was whimper.

He played with one nipple until there was a line of fire from it to her clit. Then he switched. Back and forth. And then, like he was consolidating his work, he took his mouth away from hers—which made her whimper again—lifted her shirt, and dropped his head so he could work one tight bead with his fingertips and the other with his tongue.

"What do you feel, Auburn?" It was a low, dark tease.

She moaned.

"Do you feel like you could come? If I kept doing this? What if—" he dropped a hand between her legs, cupping her through denim. She could feel the heat of his hand against the seam of her jeans, and she tipped to meet it. The friction over her clit made her cry out, and he moved his hand away, a tease. She clutched his hand and drew it back to where it had been, rubbing herself shamelessly against his palm.

"Kiss me again," she begged.

He wound her higher and higher, his mouth on hers, his fingertips relentlessly teasing the tip of her breast, his palm cupped tight where she rocked into him. The sensation was drawing into a tight knot in her low belly, so hot and sweet it was calling her name, when the breeze carried voices up the beach.

Trey pulled away from the kiss and touched his lips to her ear. Whispered, his breath tingling everywhere, "There are people walking on the beach, Auburn. Do you want me to stop?"

He had to know the answer. He'd taken her there himself.

"I—can't—"

"Let it come, Auburn. Come, baby."

The tension drew one impossible notch more taut—nipple, belly, clit, core—and he leaned in close and kissed her again, his body blocking her from the view of the passing beach walkers, shielding his hand between her thighs and his hand under her shirt, over lace, teasing, teasing. She tipped over the edge behind the screen of his body, a scream held tight in her throat, the roar of the ocean drowning all the lesser sounds—the harsh pants of his breath in her ear, the squeak she couldn't contain. The orgasm rolled through her like thunder, wave after wave of pleasure. His hand dropped away from her nipple just as it got too sensitive to bear, but the other one stayed snug against her sex, coaxing the last squeeze out of her inner muscles.

She held her breath while the people passed on, their voices fading.

"God, Trey, *God*."

"Beach magic," he murmured into her hair.

24

oly shit.

He'd suspected it would be good between them. He'd known that the chemistry would be explosive. But he hadn't been prepared for how good it would feel to make Auburn fall apart.

His dick was so hard behind the zipper of his jeans that it was taking all the self-control he had not to rock the palm of his hand against it.

Beach magic indeed.

She still had her face buried against his shirt, her body limp and relaxed in his arms. He was waiting for her to lift her face and show him the aftermath. He wanted to see her cheeks flushed with what he'd done to her. Her eyes bright and sparkling.

Instead, she pulled back from him and turned away.

Shit.

He knew that posture. Everyone knew it.

Regret.

And why was he fucking surprised? He *knew* this was crazy.

"Auburn."

"Thank you. That was amazing." Her tone was formal.

"Look at me, sweetheart. I can tell you're freaking out."

"I'm not freaking out. I'm ... confused."

He reached for her hand, and she let him take it. It was reassuring in his. Like she hadn't retreated fully, not yet.

"You want to talk about it?"

"It can't help but change things. Like it'll influence your decision about Beachcrest in some way. In some way that's bad for me," she clarified.

"Give me some credit," he said sternly. "I can separate business and sex."

She looked away from him, out at the darkness lowering over the ocean. "Of course you can. I forgot for a second who I was dealing with." Her voice was strained.

Damn it, he hadn't meant—

But if he hadn't meant that—that this was *just* sex—what did *that* mean?

"Auburn."

"It's just—I wasn't supposed to do that. I made a deal with myself. That I was going to sort myself out, get my life on track, stand on my own two feet, *before* I let anyone in my pants."

"I can't imagine you *not* standing on your own two feet," he said.

"Yeah, well, you didn't see me with Patrick."

He just couldn't picture her getting knocked backwards. She was fierce and quick and a match for any man he'd ever met, himself included. "What did he do to you, Auburn?"

She seemed to fold in on herself, and for a moment, he didn't think she was going to answer. Then she squared her shoulders. "I met him when I was working a weekend at The Nines in Portland. They were understaffed and one of my school friends called me and said they were paying double overtime for good people who could fill in."

He whistled, and a fleeting smile passed over her face, then vanished. "It was fun for a couple of days, being there, but it wasn't really my thing. Lots of entitled Silicon Vall—" She slammed her lips shut.

He laughed. "Entitled Silicon Valley assholes?"

She bit her lip and smiled sheepishly. "Let's just say a lot of guys who thought the hotel staff lived to serve them."

"Was Patrick one of them?" Although Patrick was a different brand of entitled. He was a New York I-banker who—Trey knew —had grown up Connecticut country-club rich. That was a whole other breed from the guys Trey encountered in the West Coast tech subculture. No better—but different.

"No. He actually called out one of his colleagues who was treating me like shit."

Trey felt a stab of appreciation, mixed with—well, fuck it. Envy. Because his situation with Auburn up to this point hadn't allowed him to be much of a hero. The opposite, in fact. But at least he hadn't done anything calculated to get in her pants. The Patrick Moriarty he knew from reputation was more than capable of standing up for a woman with the sole goal of getting laid. Hell, the Patrick Moriarty he knew was entirely capable of orchestrating an incident just to give himself a chance to play the hero.

You don't know that's what happened, he chastised himself.

"He asked me out. Wined and dined and totally, completely snowed me. Talk about being swept off your feet. He got us reservations at exclusive restaurants no one could get into for months. Flew me to Paris to see the Eiffel Tower. Booked us an exclusive nighttime Disney World tour. We did a long weekend in Bangkok. You get the idea."

Okay, he *really* didn't like that. The idea of Patrick Moriarty pulling out all the stops to woo Auburn ... Trey was still feeling the surge of intense power that went along with what they'd just done—the pleasure he'd given her, but the rest of it, too, the way she'd let him take charge, when she didn't let him do that in any other arena. And while he had no right to feel possessive of her, at the moment he didn't want any other man, ever, to have *swept her off her feet.*

"He asked me to move to New York. I agonized, but he was so persuasive." She frowned. "I turned my back on my family. My career. I didn't realize yet that there weren't a million other Beachcrests out there. I thought I could find something else similar. I took a couple of jobs in New York hotels—but oh, God, I *hated* those jobs. Patrick kept saying maybe hospitality wasn't for me, and I started to think he was right."

He couldn't help it; he made a strangled sound of dissent.

"I know," she said wearily. "I started taking other jobs here and there, but nothing worked out. And by then Patrick was saying, 'You don't need to work, Auburn. I want to take care of you. And eventually I got worn down.

"And it wasn't just that. We lived in his New York apartment. He had people to do everything—cooking, cleaning, shopping— so there wasn't much I could do to be useful. We almost never socialized. He said he wanted to protect me from the media and how catty people were in his social circles, and that sounded good to me. That wouldn't have been my scene. But I didn't realize how small my world was getting."

"I did a bunch of volunteer work, but he was always saying he thought people were taking advantage of my good nature. He was very loving but also very possessive, so if I spent time with people other than him, it made him jealous. So—"

She closed her eyes.

"So I stopped. I stopped visiting my siblings because it made him so unhappy for me to leave for four or five days at a time, and he was always too busy with work to fly to the West Coast. You see where this is going, don't you?"

He nodded. His stomach was knotted up from the effort of not cursing out Patrick Moriarty.

"Chiara had tried to tell me from the beginning that he was bad news, and toward the end, she stepped it up, until—I stopped calling her or taking her calls. Because it felt like I had to choose between Chiara's view of things and Patrick's, and I couldn't believe that Patrick, who loved me so much, would—"

She made a small choking sound, and he reached for her, but she pulled away. "Chiara came to New York. She tried to basically do an intervention. Point out to me what had happened, what I'd given up, what I'd become. And I told her to get the hell out, to go away and not come back."

Her shoulders were shaking, but her voice was still steady. Strong.

"It happened so slowly. That's my only defense. My world got smaller and smaller and smaller until he filled the whole thing, and I didn't notice because he never hurt me. He wasn't emotionally abusive. He was so careful, so subtle, the way he controlled me. He never even really gaslit me. Not until near the end, when I finally admitted I was unhappy and he made it all about me. About how I didn't know how to be happy or how to see the good in things. He said I'd always let Chiara control me and that she was still trying to manipulate me because she was jealous of my relationship with him. And a lot of other bullshit. He played me like a violin."

"But you left him. In the end."

She took a deep breath. "I did. It was Beachcrest that saved me, to be perfectly honest. Carl called me. He said he'd fired yet another crappy manager and that the job was open. He knew it was longer than a long shot ..."

Tears were running down her face, and his fingers ached with the need to wipe them away. He knew *he* wasn't the one who'd made her cry—but it still hurt like a mofo.

"I wouldn't have come home for Chiara. Or any of my siblings. Or Carl, even. But something about Beachcrest needing me gave me the courage to take a really hard look at where I was and how different it was from where I'd meant to be. I hated what I saw. I finally saw what Chiara saw, and heard what she'd been trying to tell me. I can't even explain why. Maybe I was just ready. But what I know is, Beachcrest brought me home."

The truth of what Patrick had done to Auburn made his stomach hurt. He'd hidden her away from the world and systematically taken away all the things that mattered to her. Auburn thrived on people, glowed with the joy she got out of them. If she'd been his, instead of Patrick's, he would have wanted to watch her meet someone new every day. Not kept her locked up like some kind of exotic bird in a—

In a gilded cage.

His thought train screeched to a stop like a needle skidding on a record. Was he really any better than Patrick? Hadn't he done almost exactly that to Karina? Wasn't he *still* trying to do it to Brynn and Carl?

"So you see," she said. "I lost myself in that relationship. I lost track of who I was, what I needed. And that's why I vowed to figure out all those things first, before—" She sighed. "Look. That—" she gestured to encompass what had just passed between them. "—was amazing. I want to do it again. I want to do it again right fucking now. And I want you to get yours." She gave him a sexy smirk that breathed new life into his dick, which had just calmed down. "But—with Patrick, I didn't know what I was getting into. I didn't see how the sex was all caught up with money and power. In this situation? I already know it. And I'd be an idiot—" She took a deep breath. "This *can't* happen again."

He wanted to cry out that it didn't have to be that way. That he wasn't Patrick.

But he could also hear Karina's voice in his head. *I've tried,*

Karina had said. *I've tried so hard. To make you see me. To make you listen. To make you understand what I need. But it's all about money to you. It's all about work. You're like King Midas. Everything you touch turns to gold, including all the people you're supposed to love.*

He shook his head, to ward it off. Brush it away.

Karina was right. Auburn was right.

He *was* about money. He was about this sale. He was about saving his business. There was no other way out. And he couldn't have both.

Slowly, grudgingly, he nodded. "You're right."

"Shit," she said, and for a second he thought she was referring to the substance they'd just landed themselves in, until she yanked her phone out of her pocket and peered at it. "One of the guests is having a crisis and Luz needs backup, so I have to get back. Help me put the fire out?"

It took him a moment to realize she meant the literal blaze in front of them. They smothered it with water and stones, and he helped her wheel the cart back up to the inn.

"Can I help with the crisis?" he asked, when they reached the shed and she'd stowed the wheelbarrow.

She grinned at him. "As much as it would give me sick pleasure to make you wield the steam cleaner, I don't think it's going to improve your opinion of Beachcrest if I bring you with me. It's the less glamorous side of the gig, I'm afraid. One of the kids just threw up." She sighed. "Happens almost every time we have kids at a hotdog roast. They don't know their own capacity when it comes to marshmallows." She shrugged. "I'm used to it. You're off the hook."

"Thanks," he said, laughing.

He had turned to go, when she called him back.

"Trey. Thank you. And—I'm usually all for reciprocating, it's just—"

"No," he said. "That was—" He didn't know how to say what

he felt. That even though things couldn't keep going that way between them, he in no way, shape, or form could regret what had just happened. "That was for you. You owe me nothing. I'd hate it if you thought that."

"Well. Thank you."

He parted ways from her, went back to his room, flopped down on the bed.

And found himself, idiotically, impossibly, ridiculously, wishing he'd gone with her to help with cleanup.

Who are you, and what have you done with Trey Xavier?

It was just three days ago that everything had been so clear. That it had made perfect sense. That he had known what he needed to do and how to do it.

Cleaning up vomit was no one's idea of a good time, that was for sure. But if he'd gone with her, he'd be *with her*. And he'd know exactly what he was supposed to do next.

As it was, his emotions were a mess, and he had no idea where to start with the cleanup.

25

B rynn and the boys found him setting up beach chairs for parade viewing on a stretch of Main Street sidewalk. Auburn had sent him ahead, an advance guard, to stake out the territory for Beachcrest guests.

"You've got a lot of explaining to do," Brynn said.

He gave her his best innocent wide-eyed look.

"Don't bullsh—" She shot a look toward her boys. "Don't yank my chain. You know what I mean. Beach fire. Marshmallows. Hot dogs. And now you're watching a parade, and you're *cheerful about it*. It's her, isn't it? Auburn."

"I don't know what you're talking about."

"Boys, you see the Starbucks over there? Take this money and get yourselves a snack, okay?" Brynn handed his nephews cash and turned back to him as soon as they took off. Her too-sharp eyes scraped over him, and there was nowhere to hide. "You like her!"

That, too, was spoken in the tone of an accusation, and there was no point in denying it. He didn't even try.

She was obviously completely delighted with this turn of events. "So *that's* what the hot dog roast thing was all about. And you inviting me and the boys to watch the parade in front of Beachcrest."

He shook his head. "No. This has nothing to do with that. Carl and I cut a deal—he'd let me sell Beachcrest if I spent a week letting her show me Beachcrest's finer features—"

"And she turned out to be one of its finest!" Brynn burst out.

"You're having way too much fun with this."

"I just haven't seen you enjoying yourself like you did last night since before Mom died," she said.

That shut them both up for a minute—as any mention of their mother's death did—but Brynn was irrepressible. "I couldn't figure out why you were suddenly acting like a real human being. But it's because you got roped into it. I knew there had to be money on the line somehow or other."

That hurt—but since it was true enough—there *was* money on the line—he didn't dispute it.

"But that doesn't explain why you seem to be genuinely having a good time."

"No," he said, fighting a smile. "It doesn't."

She stared at him for a long time. "Well," she said. "Well, well, well."

"Don't get too excited. It can't happen. Believe me. I spent most of last night trying to figure it out, and—she and I? It's just not an option."

"Because you're going to tear down her inn."

She said it matter of factly, but the voice that spoke up behind him was anything but matter of fact.

"He is, the ass! He's—Trey, you've turned into someone I don't even know."

He turned to find Carl there, a little hunch-shouldered—the surgery scars were still bothering him—but otherwise more or less himself. For better or for worse...

"I didn't teach you to do business the way you're doing it

now. Fighting dirty with the people you care about. Selling to the highest bidder even if there's someone else who needs it more—"

"Grandpa, you just got out of the hospital," Brynn said. "This isn't the time or the place—"

"I do business exactly the way you taught me to," Trey said stiffly.

"Trey, walk away," Brynn said.

"Bullshit," Carl said. "I taught you that when being a good human conflicted with being a good businessperson, you should always be a good human."

"What you forgot," Trey said coldly, "is that when other people are depending on you, being a good businessperson is the best way to be a good human."

Carl pinned him with eyes that despite being bloodshot and a little rheumy, were still a piercing gray. His mother's eyes, and his own. "You think I should have helped your parents out. You think if I hadn't thrown good money after bad so many times, I could have kept your mother from working herself to—so hard."

Trey acknowledged the truth of that with a tight nod.

"Regardless of what you said the other day in my hospital room, Trey, I know I disappointed you. And if I have one regret in life, it's that. You didn't deserve to see another role model screw up on your watch. But you're wrong about one thing. I did try to give your parents money. Your father wouldn't take it. He was too proud and stubborn."

He heard the whoosh of air leaving Brynn's lungs, but he couldn't breathe in *or* out.

"That was his worst crime, Trey. Not being foolish. Being stubborn. And even though I may not have been the businessman you wanted me to be, I think I can say I *was* the man I wanted to be. If you tear down Beachcrest, will you be able to say the same?"

The truth of it hit him, then. He was going to tear down Auburn's inn. He *was*. Because through all of this, he'd never wavered in that conviction. He'd agreed to their deal because it was good business for him to do so. He'd kept his word and followed through on his half of the bargain because that was what he did. He'd heard her out and seen what she'd had to show him. But he'd never intended to change his mind.

Meanwhile, she'd broken through his defenses. She'd gotten him to talk—about his childhood, his father, even Karina. She'd heard about parts of him that he hid from the world. She'd made him break his own rules, turned him upside down so giving her pleasure felt more important than chasing his own. She'd made him laugh, and she'd made him feel alive.

And he was going to reward her by leveling her fucking inn to the ground.

If he did, there would be no more jockeying for position, no more banter, no more shopping together, no more conversations, no more bike rides—

No more Auburn coming apart in his arms, giving herself over to him with complete and total trust.

"Sit *down*, Carl!" Auburn said, suddenly there beside him, cheerful and buoyant. She was wearing the sexiest little sundress he'd ever seen. White with yellow flowers. Teeny-tiny spaghetti straps. A short and flirty skirt. He wanted to flip it up and see what she was wearing underneath.

"I've been sitting and lying down for *days*," Carl grumbled.

"Which is exactly right for someone who's just had a heart attack," Brynn said, coming back to life again and settling their grandfather into a lawn chair.

Auburn tried to tuck a blanket around him, but he pushed her off. "Over my cold dead body!"

"Don't say that," Brynn shushed.

"I'm just reminding you that I can always exercise my prerog-
ative to die if you give me a hard time."

Auburn gave him a fond, exasperated slap on the shoulder
and left the blanket on the ground next to him as she passed out
Ziploc bags to Tyler and Jake, who'd returned from Starbucks
and joined the growing crowd on the curb. "For candy," she said.
"If it's okay with your mom."

She'd brought tubes of sunscreen, too, and water bottles,
and blankets for the kids to sit on until the parade started. The
fishermen came out and sat in beach chairs side by side. They
were in good moods, bargaining with the boys for a share of the
candy haul, teasing Auburn about having served granola that
morning, a sub-par breakfast experience. Dewann put an arm
around Rick's shoulder and left it there.

An older couple came up the sidewalk and stopped to talk to
Auburn. After a moment, the man—sixty-something, with side-
burns that were only one step removed from mutton chops—
drew Auburn aside, and they stood and talked for a few minutes.
Whatever the subject, it was serious; he could tell from the set of
both their shoulders. Until hers slumped.

"Can you hand me that sunscreen?" Brynn asked, and he
made himself look away from a conversation that could not
possibly be any of his business. He handed her the tube, then
helped her coat the boys—he did arms and she did faces.

He saw that Auburn's conversation had finished up. She was
standing still, staring into the distance, and he didn't like her
expression. Like someone had told her that her dog had died.
He wanted immediately to put his arms around her—but he
wasn't sure how that would fly. Or how he would explain it to
Brynn, who was watching him with sharp eyes.

He walked over to where Auburn stood. "Who was that?"

She could have told him it was none of his business, but she
said, "Keegan Horan. A VP at Tierney Bay Bank and Trust. And

the bearer of bad news. No jumbo mortgage for me." She said it lightly, but he could see how much it bothered her. She sighed, heavily.

"What does that leave?"

"Diana Cooper. Bootstrap. Or getting help from family or friends."

Some emotion was rising in his chest, hot and fierce. "Not Patrick Moriarty. For God's sake."

She crossed her arms, and the sucked-a-lemon look deepened, as did the furrows in her brow. "In what version of the universe is that your choice? After you put me in this situation?"

Suddenly they were squared off, across a gulf as wide as the one that had opened that first afternoon in Carl's hospital room. He glared, and she glared back, and it was like they were the only two people in all of Tierney Bay—no chairs lining main street, no kids waving flags, no dogs wagging tails, no blue and white t-shirts and red hair ribbons. Just the two of them.

And the one thing he *did* have control of.

He knew he was about to detonate a truth bomb, that what he was going to say would change everything between them, for better or for worse.

But things had already changed between them—and even though a huge part of him still wished he'd had the strength not to touch her, not to complicate this already fraught situation, there was no avoiding that fact.

"No," he said. "I can't make you refuse Patrick's money. But the rest of it really is my decision. I decide whether or not I sell you Beachcrest. This has all been a cute game, but it's my call what happens next, and that's the bottom line."

Her mouth fell open, and he braced for impact.

26

S he felt suffocated, suddenly, and the image that came into her head was the apartment where she'd lived with Patrick. Expensively decorated with furniture, paintings, and knickknacks that had been chosen by someone else. Big enough to put all of Beachcrest's square footage inside it, and yet so goddamn small that by the end she hadn't been able to breathe at all. Her own gilded cage.

She wasn't an idiot. She knew what was happening. She'd let things get physical with Trey and now he felt territorial. And he would happily piss on whatever he needed to piss on to keep her from turning to Patrick—not that she'd had the slightest intention of doing so. But he hadn't asked, had he?

"You'd do that," she said. "You'd snatch Beachcrest away from me, renege on our deal before it's even done, just because you're having a dick-measuring match in your head with some guy from my past."

She should have known better than to give any piece of herself to him. Now he was doing what men—what rich and powerful men—did in these situations. He was using his money and his power to control whatever he could control—and in this case, that was her.

And she was so fucking disappointed in him she couldn't speak.

But mostly, she was disappointed in herself. For letting him feel like he had any right to make decisions for her—

"No!" he said.

"What?"

"No. You misunderstood me. I'm not talking about reneging. Or snatching anything away from you. The opposite in fact. I'm saying—"

He swallowed, hard.

"Auburn. There's something I need to tell you."

A fist squeezed in her belly, a warning that whatever it was, she probably wasn't going to like it.

"Do you know what 'overleveraged' means?"

She shook her head.

"It's when a company has taken on too much debt."

"Okay," she said uncertainly.

"My company. Home Base. It's overleveraged."

The words came out slowly, as if they pained him. He closed his eyes, and an expression like grief came over his face. It took her a moment to recognize it for what it was.

Shame.

"Trey."

He opened his eyes but wouldn't meet her gaze. "We had more than half a billion on the balance sheet. Operating budget for two decades. Everyone thought it was a good time to grow. So we did. And then something that was too big to fail failed, and we were locked up in it, and overnight we went from being able to meet our obligations for five-to-ten years to being able to meet them for less than two months."

She was starting to see. And her stomach hurt. Not so much

for her—although she was getting the sense of how his revelations would affect her—but for him. She didn't think many people knew what he'd just told her. She didn't think Trey Xavier would admit what he was admitting to most people in the world.

But he was telling her.

As scared as she was, as bad as this news was, she was warm all over, and she wanted, more than anything, to reach out and hug him. *Hold* him.

God, how had she gotten here? And—how did she get herself *out* again?

"I scrambled, trying to find a way out. I found a buyer, which was a miracle in and of itself. It's a good buyer, a good sale. If I make the sale, I'll come out a winner instead of a loser. I'd be able to start another company—instead of not knowing if I can keep my house and my car. And chances are good that my people—a hundred and fifty employees, to be exact—could keep their jobs. But to make that deal go through, to make that sale, I have to be able to keep the company running long enough for the deal to get penned and signed."

He took a deep breath. "I'm just a few weeks short of money. That's it. Just a few weeks. Nothing in the scheme of things. Except..." He closed his eyes. "Everything is leveraged. *Everything.*"

Slowly, slowly, the last piece fell into place for Auburn. "Everything except Beachcrest."

"*Even* Beachcrest. It's mortgaged almost to the hilt, thanks to my grandfather. Which means—"

"That the only thing you can do is sell it."

He closed his eyes again, and she could see the pain etched into his features.

"The last thing I wanted, you have to believe me, is to sell it out from under him. God." His tone was fervent. "But then he had the heart attack, and he said he was ready to retire, and I thought—here's a way out. It was like being handed my salvation, Auburn—"

"And then I came along."

A funny expression came over Trey's face then. "Yes. And then you came along."

"And ruined everything."

"That's not—that's not what I was going to say."

His eyes were warm on her face, and if she hadn't been so confused, she would have stepped toward him. Let herself be pulled into the tenderness of his gaze.

But she *was* confused.

"If you don't get the money—?"

He sighed. "A hundred and fifty people lose their jobs. I lose my business and—well, most of the money in it."

She thought of what he'd built, and from what. A lemonade stand, a pet-sitting business. Lawnmowing, landscaping, house flipping, real estate development, his own app ... bit by bit, one thing building on the next, each increment taking him further from the *shithole* of his childhood. Leaving behind his father's world.

She thought about what he'd said about his dad. *And he flailed—broke shit, ruined shit. Couldn't hold a job. Then he'd get into these risky schemes to try to make the money he couldn't make nine-to-five.*

And then she thought about Beachcrest and her mind stalled out.

"If I get Beachcrest ... you lose everything."

He opened his eyes. They were clear and bright. "No. Not *necessarily.*"

"But I don't—how—"

And then she got it.

"You could sell it to me."

"I could sell it to you," he affirmed. "But—"

She was there, a beat ahead of him. "But only if I have the money."

He heaved a sigh. "Yes."

"Which I don't. Trey?"

"Uh-huh?"

"Why are you telling me this now?"

"Because you won. By the book. You made me fall for Beachcrest. And because—" He hesitated. "Because it didn't feel right anymore. After what happened between us on the beach. And after what you told me about Patrick and how he'd controlled you. I had to give you a fair shot."

"But that's all it is. A fair shot. If I can't get the money, you'll sell to ...?"

"If you can't get the money, I have to sell to someone else." His eyes met hers, and she thought the worry there was as much for her, and what she stood to lose, as for himself. "I've called in every favor I have coming to me already. If I thought I could squeeze another ten thousand out of anyone I knew, believe me, I'd do it."

"I believe you," she said quietly. "How much time do we have?"

"Monday. I've done the math a hundred ways, and—well, Tuesday, if the Dow doesn't lose more than a hundred points."

She didn't let her shock and horror show; he didn't need her to pile onto the shame and fear he was already feeling. "Okay. Let me think. There's still one more lender who has to get back to me. And Chiara set up a Bootstrapper page for me. But when I checked this morning, there were only a thousand dollars in pledges. That's hardly going to save our asses."

"I have a friend who's gotten some good startups off the ground with cloud-sourced money. I can have him look at what you've got on the page, tweak it a bit, advise you about advertising. That's a favor I can still call in."

She nodded.

"And Auburn?"

She found him looking at her intently, an expression she couldn't quite read on his face. "Mmm?"

"It wasn't jealousy. The thing with Patrick. I mean—" The corner of his mouth turned up, that rare Trey smile that she'd already learned to crave. "Like any sane man would, I wish I were the only person who'd ever felt you come apart in his arms—"

She made a small involuntary sound, somewhere between a gasp and a whimper, and his smile brightened another notch.

"But I meant what I said. I don't want you to take his money, because—because I have nothing but respect for the fact that you walked away from him. And the last thing I want is for you to have to turn to him."

She couldn't believe—couldn't *believe*—that she'd thought him icy or power hungry or *like Patrick* in any way, and she was about to say so when an eardrum splitting *honk*—the firetruck going by—made her jump. The parade was passing them now, and she turned to watch for a moment as the firefighters tossed saltwater taffy and other candy toward the curb, and Trey's nephews and her two young guests dove after it. When she turned back toward him, he was watching the parade, too, and his smile had bloomed into a disbelieving grin. "Is that a *lawn chair twirling* group?"

"Indeed," she said.

"If I were not already in love with Beachcrest and Tierney Bay, I would be now." He turned the grin on her, and she felt a little weak in the knees at the wattage of full-on Trey amusement.

She caught her breath, rallied her sanity, and said, "We're going to figure this out. We are."

"We," he repeated.

"Yes. We."

His gaze found hers and held, and held. There was so much warmth there that for a moment she lost all sense of time and place—she just wanted to turn herself over to it. Then his face cracked with mischief. "If you can stop fighting with me long enough for us to work together."

27

A s the parade goers drifted back to Beachcrest for the afternoon's barbecue, Trey and Auburn hid in the lobby and called Trey's friend James, the cloud-sourcing expert.

"You need better incentives," James said bluntly, as soon as Auburn was done explaining the situation and the need for speed.

They spent a while brainstorming, and Trey multitasked on his email, calling in what he described as "the last favors left on earth" to get some of his business buddies to donate subscriptions and services.

"Who's going to support some inn in Oregon because they want a Home Base subscription? Or cloud computing services?" Auburn demanded.

"It's a long shot," James admitted. "But it's better than what you've got there. You need people willing to give five hundred dollars. Or a thousand. Ideally? More."

When he put it like that, it made Auburn's stomach curl in despair.

James frowned on screen. "The real key is how you get the

word out. I'd suggest running both Bootstrapper and social media ads. Hundreds of dollars a day of each, if possible."

"It's possible," Auburn said.

"Are you good with creative?" James asked.

"Creative?"

"The design for the ads."

"Um—yes?" Auburn hazarded, shooting Trey a look.

He nodded. "My assistant can do them."

Thank you, she mouthed.

James ended the phone call shortly after that, and Auburn hung up and buried her face in her hands.

"Don't," Trey said. "Please. Don't give up. It's only Thursday."

"Or, if you look at it from a different perspective, it's already Thursday," she said.

"Don't give up on what?" Chiara said from the doorway.

"Nothing," Trey and Auburn said at the same time.

Chiara rolled her eyes. "Seriously, people? Do you know me, Auburn? That kind of shit never flies with me."

Auburn looked at Trey, and he gave a slight nod of assent.

"Trey's willing to sell me Beachcrest," Auburn said. "But I still need to raise the money."

"Why can't you just finance her?" Chiara demanded.

Trey opened his mouth to answer, but a voice cut in before he could speak.

"Finance her for what?"

It was Mason, who'd wandered in from the barbecue.

"Hey, Mace," Chiara said.

"Hey. I couldn't take it out there."

Auburn and Chiara both knew what he meant. Mason was—well, some people said he was shy. Some said he was quirky. Auburn thought he was the sweetest, most loyal human being on earth, and if the rest of the world couldn't see it, fuck 'em. But parties were definitely not his scene. In general, conversation with humans other than his siblings was not his scene.

And yet Mason had once let slip that he was a regular and devoted user of Swiperight, which Auburn wondered the heck out of. How did you manage hookup culture without having to talk to strangers? Or maybe that was exactly why he thrived at hookup culture ...

"Mason, this is Trey Xavier. He's Carl's grandson. Trey, this is my brother, Mason."

Trey came forward, hand out for a shake, but Mason only acknowledged him with a slight nod, and Trey let his hand drop.

She'd have to explain her youngest brother to Trey later.

He leaned on the counter. "What are you guys doing?"

"Working on Auburn's Bootstrapper page."

"What does Auburn need a Bootstrapper page for?"

That was Levi, who suddenly manifested in the doorway to the office.

Oh, *shit.*

Chiara shot a look Auburn's way. Which clearly said, *You didn't tell him?*

Auburn closed her eyes and hoped her siblings would go away, but when she opened her eyes, far from having disappeared, they'd magnetically attracted Hannah, their youngest sister. "What are you guys all doing in here? The meat is coming off the grill, and it looks ah-maaaazing." Then she caught the vibe of the room and froze. "What's going on?"

No. This was not happening.

Auburn looked at Trey—who seemed shell-shocked at the sight of all of her siblings gathered in one place.

"Levi, Hannah, this is Trey. He's Carl's grandson. Trey, Levi is my big brother, and Hannah is the youngest."

"I'm lots of things besides the youngest," Hannah pointed out grumpily.

"The most beautiful, the smartest, and the least modest," Chiara said, poking her little sister. Hannah poked back.

"It's a pleasure to meet you," Trey said, shaking Hannah's hand, and then Levi's.

Levi was frowning. Hard. "What does Auburn need a Bootstrapper page for?" he repeated.

It was only a matter of time until Levi got his answer, Auburn knew. Easier to just give it to him upfront. "I'm going to buy Beachcrest from Trey and Carl."

"But she needs to raise the down payment," Chiara said. She shot Auburn a glance that clearly said: *We've unleashed the big brother beast.*

Levi swore under his breath. "You should have told me."

His expression was fierce. He had one of those male faces that was hewn from stone. If Auburn didn't know firsthand how much he loved her, she'd be scared of him. She figured he terrified most women—which would account for why he didn't date.

That and the fact that dating would require him to take time for himself. Away from Cape House and the responsibilities that rode on his shoulders. And Levi had turned self-sacrifice into a fine art and a way of life.

When Auburn was a pre-teen, Levi had been a pretty fun guy. A bit of a partier, in fact. Auburn often wondered if that part of him still existed in there, buried deep under the seriousness.

"You *know* why I didn't tell you," Auburn said quietly.

They stared at each other for a long moment, during which the stubborn streak they'd inherited from their father burned in two sets of blue eyes. Then Levi looked away.

"If I hadn't just done the renovations, Cape House would have cash," he said, and Auburn could see the unhappiness behind his eyes. "But right now? I could maybe eke out another $25K. And it's yours, for what it's worth."

"No way," Auburn said. "That money isn't just for you and Cape House. It's for all of us."

Levi—and Cape House—had put them all through college, paid their medical expenses, taken care of them through every possible bit of life drama. It had been the roof over all their heads at one time or another.

And Auburn, no matter how much she loved Beachcrest, knew Cape House came first. Protecting Cape House was paramount, at least until Hannah went to college in two years.

"I've got some financing possibilities lined up," Auburn said.

"Tell me it's not Patrick," Levi said fiercely.

Trey shot an appraising gaze in Levi's direction.

"Not Patrick," Auburn said quickly.

"What about him?" Levi tipped his head in Trey's direction.

"I'm not in a position to do that," Trey said.

Levi gave a tight nod at that. "You want to sell and get out."

"I do."

"There's one lender who's, um, interested," Auburn said. "Interested" was definitely too strong a word, but she wasn't sure how riled up she wanted to get Levi right now. "But Kee and I thought we'd do this Bootstrapper thing as a Plan B."

"I've got a little saved," Mason said, startling them.

They all turned to look at him.

"Fifteen thousand."

"Holy *shit*, Mace," Auburn said.

He shrugged. "Was thinking about getting myself a place. But it can wait. I know you're good for it, sis."

"No." Auburn didn't even hesitate. "I won't take it. It's time for you to have a place of your own."

She could feel Chiara's murmured assent. Auburn didn't delude herself that owning a house would fix everything troubled in Mason, but it would at least help. Give him something to care for, or about. He'd been fourteen when their parents had died, and he'd never fully rallied.

"I've got ten," Chiara said.

Auburn shook her head. "No. No to all of you. I'm going to do this some other way. I'm going to figure it out, but I'm not going to figure it out by stealing from your dreams."

"My twenty-five is yours, though," Levi said. "It's investment money, and I think Beachcrest is a good investment, especially with you at the helm. I never thought Carl managed it as well as he could, but I know you would. I know you'll pay me back."

Her eyes filled with tears. Hearing him say that meant a lot to her. She and Levi had spent hundreds of hours talking business over the years; she'd been the closest thing he'd had to a partner and trusted advisor, and until she'd gone to college, she'd learned everything she knew about hotel management from him. He was a great businessman—so his praise? It felt damn good.

"Thank you," she whispered.

It was less than a tenth of what she'd need—and she hadn't told them, for very good reasons, that she had to have it by Monday—but it was an act of faith she'd craved without knowing it.

"Do you think this Bootstrapper thing'll work?" Levi asked.

"We just added a bunch of incentives. We had a one-night stay, but Trey got some of his buddies to chip in other motivations."

"Very good of you, dude, given that she's buying the thing from you," Levi said.

"Well," Trey said, looking pained. "I, um, have strong reasons to want to make the sale to her. It was my granddad's business, and I know she'll do right by it."

"You need a couple of other levels, too," Levi pointed out. "You want to get the small donors, not just the big ones. You'd be surprised how much those add up. I did a Kickstarter a couple of years ago to run a Tierney Bay Warner Brothers Cartoon Marathon—" he explained to Trey. "The small donors ended up giving more than half the total. You need, like, Beachcrest T-shirts and tote bags. I've got some outstanding credit at Zazzle—"

"Flipflops and beach towels and sunglasses," Hannah interrupted, with all the certainty of a teenager.

"You can give away a few weekends at Cape House if it helps," Levi said.

"And something with sand," Hannah said. "Sand from Tierney Bay's beach. Like those little sand globes with teeny tiny shells in them they sell at Sea Shoppe. I'll make them."

"I'll help," Chiara said.

"Me too."

It was Mason's gruff and unexpected words that finally made Auburn's eyes fill with tears.

"You *guys*," she said.

"There's no crying in baseball," Levi said, eyeing her. "Can this wait an hour? The meat is off the grill and it looks—" he shot Hannah a teasing glance—"ah-maaaazing."

28

"Your family is terrific," Trey said.

She smiled. "They are."

Her family had gone on ahead to the party while he and Auburn made some last tweaks to the Bootstrapper page and set up a few ads. When they were ready to rejoin the party, they walked toward the front of the inn and he held the door open for her.

"Your brothers and sisters are going to hate me so much when they find out the real situation."

"They *know* the real situation," she said. "You've offered to sell me Beachcrest, and I'm going to buy it."

"Unless you can't raise the money by Monday, in which case I'm going to sell it out from under you and ruin your life plans."

"Let's not go there," she said. "This is the beach. Beach magic is in full effect. It's going to work itself out."

He thought of her saying, "It's not that kind of magic," but didn't call it out. He didn't want to corrupt her July 4th cheer with his hardheadedness. The fact that she'd already been turned down by one of the two lenders who'd seemed willing to consider her proposition boded ill, and James's use of the term "long shot" had left a bad taste in his mouth.

They went down the front steps and around the side of the inn. The festivities were in full swing. Long tables groaned under the weight of food—some cooked in the inn's kitchen, but much of it catered by Auburn's brother's hotel, and the staff produced plate-loads of burgers and dogs on gas grills. People— a sea of them, red, white, and blue—flowed around the yard and up and down the sandy path to the beach, chatting and laughing and clutching plastic drink cups.

Trey eyed the yard. It was charming, actually, the grass tufts in their sandy foothold rolling down to real low dunes with longer beach grass. And the flower gardens—they were unruly, true, but in the style of Auburn's hair, wild and beautiful. He reached out and plucked a daisy and tucked it into her curls. Surprise flashed in her eyes, and she froze under his touch. He drew his hand back quickly, but not before he heard her sharp intake of breath.

He wasn't sure where today's revelations left them. He only knew he didn't want to be Patrick. "Sorry—"

"No. It's okay," she said quickly.

There was both interest and caution in her expression. She was very still, her eyes moving over his face, falling to his mouth. A wave of heat rolled through him.

And of course, just then, his phone vibrated and tolled in his pocket.

She stepped back.

Damn it.

He pulled it out. Doug. *Shit.* This was going to be one hell of a call. "I have to get this," he said apologetically. He swiped the call and headed for the edge of the party, where he leaned against one of the porch pillars. "Hey, Doug."

"Any news, man?"

"I think I have a solution that will take care of our problems."

"Yeah?" Doug said eagerly. "I like the sound of that."

"I'm going to sell the inn to Auburn Campbell."

He heard Doug take a breath on the other end of the phone. "As in, the woman who's been making your life miserable since you got there?"

"She'll quit making my life miserable if I sell her the inn."

"True," Doug said. "True enough. She have the financing lined up? Because you don't have time to fuck around. And the Royal Life Group people are going to be *pissed*. You'll have burned that bridge to the ground and then some. They've been calling me twice a day to try to get the deal inked."

"I can't afford to worry about that," Trey said. He had managed, somehow, not to answer Doug's other question, but Doug was too smart for that kind of evasion.

"The financing, Trey," Doug said quietly.

"Not yet, but—"

"Then I'm not going to burn the Royal Life bridge yet," Doug said. "Let's call it Plan B. If she doesn't get the financing—"

"She'll get the financing," Trey said shortly.

There was a long silence on the other end of the phone.

"Xavier."

"Yes?"

"Who is this woman?"

"She's—"

"Are you fucking her?"

Trey squeezed his phone so tight he could feel it flex. "No. *Asshole*."

"Do you wish you could fuck her?"

"Step the fuck off, Doug."

"Because when I said everyone had a price, I didn't mean you should sell your body."

Trey took a deep breath. Losing his temper with Doug, who

wanted the same thing Trey did, wouldn't help anything. "She's the reason my grandfather won't back down. That's what this is about. It's about doing what's simplest and most expedient. Selling to her is the fastest, most elegant solution to a complicated problem."

He'd never lied to Doug before.

That last part was true. But it wasn't the whole reason he was selling to Auburn. It wasn't even the biggest reason he was selling to Auburn.

He was selling to her because he couldn't bring himself to hurt her.

At the other end of the phone, Doug, who was no idiot and knew Trey as well as anyone on earth, took another deep breath.

"There are a hundred and fifty jobs at stake here, Xavier, including mine," Doug said. "You'll excuse me if I'm not exactly feeling secure about the way things are going over there."

"You don't need to worry."

The thought of it—of Auburn not getting the money, of Auburn not getting Beachcrest—made him sick—but Doug was right. There were a hundred and fifty human beings at the other end of this deal.

"I'll call you when I have news," he said gruffly, and ended the call.

29

Trey came back to where she stood, loading her plate with side dishes, carefully framing her burger. She was ravenous. She hadn't managed to eat breakfast this morning—trying to get Beachcrest's breakfast served, setting up for the parade, the Bootstrapper thing—time had gotten away from her.

"Everything okay?" she asked him.

He nodded.

Auburn's emotions were high. It was the excitement of the party, for sure. All the red, white, and blue, the cheerful, drunk partygoers, the free-flowing beer and wine, the tables laden with food, the smell of charbroiled meat.

And of course it was her family, and their heartfelt offers to help. She still felt a little weepy, in the best possible way, thinking of the lengths they would go to protect one another.

But she was old enough and had been around the block enough times to know that it was also *this*. His eyes on her face, hot and intent. The flower—still in her hair—and how she'd felt that innocent little caress in every cell of her body.

How he'd touched her the other night on the beach.

His willingness to back off when she'd told him about Patrick, but even more than that, what he'd said about it.

I meant what I said. I don't want you to take his money, because —because I have nothing but respect for the fact that you walked away from him. And the last thing I want is for you to have to turn to him.

The fact that he was going to sell her Beachcrest.

(*He's going to* try *to sell you Beachcrest.*)

"Uncle Trey! Uncle Trey!"

There was an explosion of small-boy activity around their knees, Trey's nephews pulling on his hands and trying to convince him to do a wheelbarrow race on the beach with them. Hannah was in charge of the party games; Auburn could see her mingling with the guests and recruiting anyone willing to participate.

"I'll do Tyler, if your Mom can do Jakey."

Brynn was shaking her head. "I did something to my back. There's no way I can bend over like that."

"I'll do Jake. If he'll let me? Will you, Jake?" Auburn asked. Brynn's youngest was six-ish, gray-eyed and earnest, with unruly hair that fell over one eye. Auburn imagined Trey must have looked a little like that, as a boy.

"Okay?" Jake agreed uncertainly.

They followed Hannah—who was the Pied Piper, kids trailing behind her in a chain—down to the beach and gathered near the start line. She'd set up two cones to be the finish. Tyler and Jake got down on their hands and knees and kicked their feet up. "Okay, Jake," Auburn said, stealing a glance at Trey. "We're going to win this. Your brother and Uncle Trey don't have the kind of teamwork it takes for an operation like this. You and I? We're golden."

"Are you going to let her trash talk us like that, Ty?" Trey demanded. The look he gave her reminded her of their first showdown in Carl's hospital room—only now she could see the gleam of humor behind it.

"You guys are going down," Ty informed them, just as Hannah counted off, "3 ... 2 ...1 ... go!"

Auburn and Jake came out of the gate slow but sure. Having quite a bit of previous experience with wheelbarrow races in the sand, she made sure she didn't push him faster than he could move his stubby little arms on the uneven surface. Trey on the other hand, got Tyler going so fast he collapsed in a heap. By the time Ty had shaken the sand out of his hair, stopped laughing, and put his feet back in Trey's hands, Auburn and Jake were almost to the finish line.

"Slow and steady wins the race," Auburn called over her shoulder.

"We're going to win!" Jake cried.

"Don't let her win!" Ty yelled up at Trey.

Obediently, Trey tried again to speed things up, but succeeded only in dumping Ty over again, and this time, Ty's momentum brought Trey down with him. Jake, full of piss and vinegar from his win, tumbled down on top of his brother and uncle, and the three of them wrestled until they were all covered with sand.

Hannah and Chiara, who had come down to watch the race, flanked Auburn, who had retreated to a safe distance to avoid getting sand in her eyes and mouth.

"They're really *cute*," Hannah said.

"Are your ovaries okay?" Chiara whispered.

"Shut up," Auburn hissed back. But they weren't. They really weren't. They'd imploded at some point while Trey was laughing and rolling around with his nephews, small boys all over him like puppies. It was maybe fifty percent the nephew-puppies, though, and fifty percent the amount of sand in Trey's hair and on his clothes.

He got to his feet, the boys still trying to drag him back down. He shook himself off, running a hand through his hair to dislodge the rest of the sand. He was wearing a new pair of board shorts. Did that mean that at some point he'd gone into town by himself and bought more beach clothes?

"Auburn," Chiara said.

"God," Auburn said aloud. "This was not supposed to happen."

"What?" Hannah asked. "What wasn't supposed to happen?"

"I wasn't supposed to *like* him."

"No," Chiara said thoughtfully. "You weren't. It's … inconvenient, isn't it? It's always so fucking inconvenient."

30

Hannah handed Jake and Auburn their gift certificates for free O'Hearn's Ice Cream cones, and Tyler pouted at the sight.

"It's okay," Hannah said. "You can enter the three-legged race with your brother."

"But then he'll have two ice cream cones!"

"Well. But you'll have one, too."

"Mom," Ty called. Brynn had just stepped out onto the beach. "Help me 'n' Jake get ready for the three-legged race."

"Jake and me," Brynn corrected, as Hannah handed her a length of rope.

He watched her bend to tie her boys' legs together.

"What do you say?"

It was Auburn, at his shoulder, one eyebrow cocked in now-familiar challenge toward the three-legged starting line. God, she was pretty, her hair pulled back for the moment into some kind of ponytail puff, her cheeks pink, her eyes sparkling. "You know you want to!"

"You're *kidding*," he said. "I haven't run a three-legged race since I was five."

"You just ran a wheelbarrow race. This is no different."

"Except for the part where we're tied together. We're not the same height."

"Come on! You seriously need to redeem yourself after that last display."

The thought of Auburn joined to any part of his body, more than anything else, propelled him to the start line.

"You're going to run it in—that?" He took advantage of the moment to survey all the territory *not* covered by her dress—and to imagine how she would look without it.

"That's my problem, isn't it?"

With a sigh, he gave in—which pretty much described every-thing that had happened this last week, not that he really minded—and followed her to the starting line, enjoying how the dress swayed over her hips and revealed delicious thighs and strong calves.

They lined up beside Jake and Tyler and Hannah knelt and bound their legs together. He watched the loop of rope close around their ankles, but his mind was on the press of her body along the length of his. She was warm. She'd been so hot against his hand last night—

If he didn't quit this line of thinking, there would be another limb in this race. He didn't want to put the other teams at a disadvantage or anything.

Hannah yelled "3 ... 2 ... 1 ... go!"—startling him out of his thoughts—and he and Auburn took off.

They were a hot mess, laughing too hard to do anything other than yank each other along. Ten feet from the finish line, he tripped and fell, dragging Auburn down on top of him in a heap. She was all silky dress and soft curves and bare thighs and arms entangled with his.

"Oh," she whispered.

He couldn't even find enough breath for that short syllable. Not the way she felt. Not with how much he wanted to slide his hand up her leg, push away that pesky dress, and feel more of her bare skin.

"You should—probably get off me. Before I do something that would not be family friendly."

"You're already—not very family friendly," she whispered. "God, Trey," she said, moving her hip just slightly against him and making him ten thousand kinds of crazy.

"I thought you said you didn't want—"

"Yeah," she said. "I did say that. But I changed my mind."

It took every ounce of self-control he possessed to help her off him and get them both back to standing. Luckily he was so tangled in the layers of his clothes that he was still more or less presentable.

"Like, *changed your mind* changed your mind?"

Pink and breathless—which he wanted to think was as much from the full-body contact as the three-legged race—she nodded.

"Is there anywhere around here we could be alone for a few minutes?" he murmured.

"Meet me behind the bike shed."

The rope had tightened around their legs and was hard to untie. She looked down at it, then up at him. "Never really thought about three-legged races as kinky before," she whispered, and he hooted a laugh.

Working together, they unbound themselves. She managed to slip away, and he went to join her.

She was leaning against the back of the bike shed. When he rounded the corner, she put her arms out, and he stepped into them. Bent his head and kissed her, a sweet, slow sweep. He groaned at the feel of her—so soft, so wet—and the taste, already familiar. He hemmed her against the wall, their bodies not touching but so close he felt every hair rise on his skin.

"I want you so fucking much," he breathed.

She was panting, and time seemed to slow. Her head tipped back against the wall and her lips parted. Her eyes were huge. "Me too," she whispered. "I want you, too."

His mouth crashed down on hers. Not gentle, but she didn't seem to care. She clutched his head, yanked his hair. Her mouth opened without hesitation, and her tongue found his, slick and eager. He went from hard to aching. He bore down on her mouth and split her with his tongue, and all he could think about was how her flesh would part between her legs just like that when he took her.

He groaned into her mouth. She moaned and pressed back, his cock trapped between their bodies.

"Fuck, Auburn," he murmured.

"That's what I was thinking," she murmured back.

"Don't say anything you don't mean."

"I don't, as a rule." She reached for his belt.

"Not here," he said. "I want to do it right. I want to lay you down on your bed and slide into you so slowly that you beg me to finish it."

She whimpered.

He slid a hand under her dress and glided it up the skin of her belly, cupping her breast and finding a nipple with his thumb. It was drawn tight. She arched and squeaked. Then he let her go. Stepped back.

"Trey—" Her chest rose and fell rapidly, her nipples visible through the thin fabric of her dress and the lace of her bra.

"Later. I promise."

She grabbed his hand and tried to tug him back to her, but he grinned and resisted. "You don't want to miss your party."

"I want—"

"Your hair's a little mussed," he said, patting it down in the back where it had been rubbed into frizz by the shed wall.

"You're a bastard."

That made him smile.

"Yeah, well. You knew that long before you let me kiss you."

31

They lay on a blanket on the beach and watched the sky explode with fireworks overhead. They were very close, shoulders touching, her hand in his. It was not much contact at all, really, but she felt like if she rolled toward him, even a little, they might both spontaneously combust. She didn't, because there were families all around them on the beach, and she didn't trust herself to stop if he touched her for real.

"So this is how Tierney Bay does the 4th," he said. "All of this? The street dance, the beach fire, the parade, the barbecue, the fireworks?"

She smiled into the dark. "Yeah. Didn't you ever come to visit Carl on the 4th of July weekend?"

She felt, rather than saw, him shake his head beside her.

"You've been doing this every year since you grew up, huh?" he asked.

"Every year except the year my parents died. None of us wanted to celebrate that year. So we didn't. And in some ways I think that was what I grieved the most. That year, it felt like everything had ended. My parents were gone. My childhood was over. And I'd lost the part of the year that had always felt like rebirth—because in Tierney Bay the world comes back to life July 4th weekend. But not that year."

His hand tightened on hers.

"And meanwhile Levi was busy trying to run Cape House, provide for all of us, keep Mason from self-destructing. Chiara— she got her heart broken on top of everything else, and she was Hannah's security blanket. Mason was just a blank wall. You might have seen—that's him. He's—not an easy guy to know."

She took a breath. "Beachcrest and Carl were the only things in my life that kept making sense."

"Auburn."

Her name in his voice was a touchpoint. An anchor. It made her know he was listening and really hearing her. It made her think about how few people did that, really *listened and heard*.

"Oh!" she said suddenly, because the sky had lit up with a brilliant ball of gold flecks. "I love those. They're my favorites. The ones that are just showers of sparks."

She turned her head. He'd turned to look at her. His face was splintered into shadows and the play of light from the fireworks above.

He got to his knees, suddenly.

"What—oh!"

He'd scooped her up and lurched to his feet, and now was carrying her across the sand, leaving the blanket behind. She didn't care. It was one of the oldest ones, a castoff from the Beachcrest beds that had gotten too worn to be good for guests. He carried her up the path, all the way to his room. He set her down, fumbled with the door key, got the door open, and followed her inside.

When he kissed her, the world stopped. He did not kiss like the man she'd met in Carl's hospital room. He kissed like the man who'd secretly adored her biscuits and chocolate chip cookies, who'd tumbled laughing into the sand on their bike ride and wrestled his nephews like they were puppies. He kissed like sunshine and salty breezes and beach magic.

He stopped kissing her and stood just looking at her, which should have been unnerving but was so lovely, the way his gaze took her in and made all of her beautiful. Her wild hair and the sunburn under the straps of her dress, the curves she sometimes loved and sometimes hated. His hands settled on her shoulders and brushed the straps away like strands of spider web.

"This okay?"

"Hell yes."

He tugged the top of her dress down and ran a finger along the top edge of her bra, tracing the contour of the lace, making her breathless. Slowly, like they had all the time in the world, he eased the cup of her bra down, baring one breast. The hunger in his eyes made it perfect.

"Oh, *God*," he said, bending and licking. "I've wanted this since the first time I saw you."

That made her mouth so dry and her whole body go soft. Or maybe it was the sensation of his tongue, circling toward her nipple, spiraling, teasing. As if he sensed the weakening of her knees, he slipped a hand behind her and drew her toward him, his tongue finally finding the sensitive tip.

She cried out.

He groaned like she'd hurt him and seemed to lose control then. He ducked his head and took her nipple, and the suckling sensation dove all the way to her core.

"There's a zipper—"

He found the zipper at the back of her dress and the silky fabric dropped to the floor around her ankles. He stepped back and looked at her. "Jesus, Auburn, you're so beautiful."

Then he picked her up again and deposited her on the edge

of the bed. He knelt on the floor, reached for her hips, and tugged her close.

"These are pretty," he said, teasing a finger over the pale green lace of her panties. He bent and kissed her where he'd just touched her, breathing her deeply. "Mmm," he said. "You smell so fucking good."

She could feel the wetness gathering for him, and she wanted to tell him, but she was breathless and wordless. He breathed her again, then buried his nose right up against her and blew warm air onto her damp flesh. Then he licked her right through her panties, and she thought she was going to scream. She wriggled, trying to get herself closer to the heat of his breath and the caress of his tongue, but he pinned her hips and she couldn't move. He held her there, his face just a few inches from her. Then he pulled back to look at her face.

"I know I came off like an asshole," he said. "That first night. I should have just told you the truth. That I saw you kneel and help that waitress and I thought, *That's a good person.*"

He was going to take her apart. Seam by seam, molecule by molecule. He was going to make it impossible for her to hang onto herself. And she was going to let him.

"You thought that?" How would things had been different if she had known, that first night, that he had seen her that way?

His mind must have been chasing along similar pathways, because he asked, "What if I hadn't fought you? What if I'd just agreed to sell you Beachcrest when you first asked?"

"You wouldn't have. You couldn't. I didn't have the money, and you have to save your company. And at that moment, you couldn't see any other way."

"I was a stubborn asshole and I wanted to fight you because you weren't letting me have my way."

She smiled at that. "I'll grant you that, but ... If you'd just said, 'You want to buy Beachcrest? Sure. Okay,' then—well, I don't know what would have happened, but it wouldn't be this."

And it seemed unimaginable and insupportable that they would not be here. That they would not have spent the last few days coaxing each other into the open like soft-bodied sea creatures from shells, cultivating the taut *wanting* that ran all the way down the length of her body, that strained towards him.

As if he felt it too, he bent and kissed her, all along where lace met her skin. He tugged her panties to one side and stroked a finger down the length of her seam, practically making her jump off the bed. "You like that?"

"So much. Do it again."

It was his turn to groan. Then he did exactly what she'd asked. He stroked his finger down the length again, then up, bringing her wetness up to her clit and circling it, so lightly, but enough that she bucked. Then he bent and repeated the motion with his tongue, and ... "Ohhhh," she moaned.

"Is it good?" He bent and did it again, a long lick and then a tight circle. A few more circles until her clit was swollen and eager. He wiggled it with the tip of his tongue until she couldn't stop the tilt of her hips. And then he buried his face in her and kissed her relentlessly while the pressure mounted and her muscles clenched helplessly.

She was going to come—but just as she could feel the point of no return looming, he drew away, stripped his shorts and t-shirt off, and crawled up over her, dragging his erection over her now-slick pussy. She groaned and tried to rub against him, but he kept himself just out of reach. The hard muscle of his abs, his hip bone, his erection through his boxer briefs, his thigh—he wouldn't let her have anything she could get purchase on.

"Bastard," she whispered.

"You know it." He laughed wickedly and bent his head to tease a nipple with his lips. His tongue. He sucked it into his mouth, tortured it between his teeth, flicked it until she could feel the trail of electric messages drawing tight between her breast and her core. If he kept it up, she would come—

So, of course, he stopped.

He kissed her mouth, long, hot, slick kisses, so deep and sweet it felt like she was suckling his mouth, and each of those kisses felt like a crank tightening in her low belly. And then he took that away, too, and just braced himself over her. Let her look at his pecs, tight with the effort of suspending himself, his broad shoulders striped with muscle, his bulging biceps and curved triceps, and the lean, mean sinewy gorgeousness of his forearms, furred with golden half-curls. He held himself off her body so she could feel the breeze of his cock moving between her legs but not the thick contact itself, and ... *"Trey."*

"What?"

"Please. Please, please, please, please, *please.*"

He smiled. "Please *what?*"

"Please put your cock inside me."

He stood up, a slow and leisurely stretch. Eased his boxer briefs down over the swollen head of his cock like he had all the time in the world, while she panted on the bed. She would probably kill him later, but right now she was too beside herself to organize a murder. She just wanted him to satisfy her craving, fill the emptiness that had bloomed and swelled in her pussy and belly.

Also, she really liked looking at him now that he was naked. The taut swells of his pecs, the ridges of his abs, the V shape of the muscles that framed his cock. His cock itself, a darker shade than the rest of his skin, thick and ruddy and long enough to kiss his navel. It made her mouth water, especially when he dug in the drawer of his nightstand and liberated a condom, then rolled it down over himself slowly—and with supreme confidence.

"I want to watch you jerk off sometime," she surprised herself by saying. "But not now. Right now I just want you to get that thing over here."

He laughed. And did, setting a hand to each side of her head in a distinctly predatory way. He settled himself between her thighs, lowering his hips to hers, easing his length along her seam so the slickness there spread all over her and coated him. She moaned. He found her clit with his cock head and rubbed lightly, in circles. She was so primed that he had her gasping again in seconds, and as soon as he did, he slid himself home, slowly but forcefully, filling her with one stroke.

"*Now* you can come," he said. All at once, she was overwhelmed: his words; the intense sense of fullness; the bright, silvery stretch; the roll of his hips, which brought pressure down hard on her swollen clit; and the expression on his face—God! the expression on his face. Like the way he looked when he'd tasted the biscuit. Or the cookie. But times a thousand. Like he didn't know what to do with all that pleasure, like it was too much for him. And she wanted to take him with her.

"Trey," she whispered. "Is it good?"

His eyes met hers.

"How does it feel? Being inside me? Because it feels really fucking good to me. You're big. You're stretching me. You're filling me. But I bet it feels really good to you, too. Am I tight? Can you feel me squeezing you? Can you feel how wet I am?"

She couldn't take her eyes off his face, the pleasure-fierce-as-pain expression, and she saw the exact moment when he broke, his eyes dropping closed, his jaw locking tight and the tendons straining in his neck and all the way down the length of his fine, beautiful body, as he came, throbbing inside her and groaning her name. *God.* Her orgasm rolled over her, making her cry out in shock and triumph.

32

"Fuck, Auburn," he said a few minutes later, when he could talk. "That was—"

But he shouldn't be surprised. He'd known it would be like this.

"—so fucking good."

"Mmm," she murmured, against his shoulder. "It was."

With effort, he withdrew from the sweet heat of her, clutching the condom carefully, and took it into the bathroom to dispose of it. When he came back she was sprawled out on the sheets, flushed and beautiful. Her curls were spilled all over the pillows, and he realized that he'd imagined them that way the first time he'd seen her. He'd imagined *her* like this. Full and lush and generous and relaxed and unself-conscious. She hadn't even made an effort to cover herself up. He ran a hand up her leg from below her knee to where her wetness coated her thigh, and she shivered and smiled at him.

He'd had eight? nine?—yes, nine—sexual encounters since Karina had left a year ago. All impersonal, casual. He ticked them off in his mind—he could name the cities he'd traveled to, the bars where the pickups had taken place. He could name the women, even, he was pleased to note.

He hadn't wanted any of them a second time. Not even close.

He wanted Auburn again. Now.

Now and later tonight and in the middle of the night, tomorrow morning—

He made himself stop, because there was only tonight. And if they couldn't save Beachcrest, if they couldn't save Home Base ...

He couldn't imagine what losing the inn would mean to Auburn or what losing his company would mean to him.

And the scenario in which they both won felt so flimsy and unlikely.

Not to mention that she lived in a permanent vacation on the Oregon coast, and he lived in a workaholic haze in Silicon Valley.

So he wouldn't let himself think about anything except the present moment. Not when she was stretched out beside him, so curvy and relaxed and beautiful. When she'd just said *yes* in every possible way to everything he'd asked her for.

He could think of a few more things he wanted her to say yes to. Her moving lazily on top of him. Or clutching the headboard as he took her from behind.

"Are you *hard* again?"

"No." He grinned at her and put his hand on his—hardening —cock. "Maybe. Um, yes."

She lay back down, her eyes on his fist. Then his face. Then his fist.

"You like watching this?" he asked. He sure as fuck liked doing it, although his hand was neither as hot nor as tight as she'd been a few moments ago. But he *really* liked the look on her face as she watched. Her pupils had crowded out the blue of her irises, and her teeth worried her lower lip.

"Hell yes."

He stopped, and was gratified by the look of disappointment and hunger that crossed her face. A good deal was always made from a position of power. "I want to watch you first."

"What, touching myself?"

"Yeah."

She blushed, and he felt a rush of blood into his cock, like the tides answering the moon. "I don't usually do it like that."

"How do you do it?"

Long hesitation, her lip taking a beating. "Toys," she whispered, finally.

"Oh," he said. Except it was really more like, *ohhhhh.* "What kind of toys?"

"I have, um, a dildo. And a vibrator. And—"

Whatever it was, it was causing her particular trouble to say aloud.

"It's called Hello Clitty."

"It is *not*."

"It is," she affirmed. "It looks like an ear thermometer, with this little silicone nozzle and you put it right over your clit, and it's contactless. It uses air to create suction—"

All the blood bottomed out of his brain, leaving him light-headed. "I think you should go get it."

She shook her head.

"No, really. I think you should go get it right now."

It didn't require much convincing. She was already pulling on her panties and dress, and she ducked out the door only to come back within three minutes with a small tote bag. She pulled out a device that, indeed, looked *exactly* like an ear thermometer. She touched a button and it began emitting a small buzz.

"Doesn't sound very powerful."

"You'd be shocked," she said. She touched it to one of his

nipples, and he jumped. Not because he got much out of having his nipples played with, but because she was right—it packed way more of a punch than he would have guessed. He didn't have a clitoris, but he could project what it would feel like to have that thing sucking on an incredibly sensitive body part, and—

His most sensitive body part was sympathetically hard as a rock.

"I want to watch you use it."

She hesitated, but he could see she liked the idea.

"Take off your dress."

She did, and shed her pretty lace panties, too. He couldn't help himself; he reached out and cupped the soft, sweet curve of her ass. Her skin felt like silk against his palm, and impulsively, he rubbed the satiny head of his cock against her. She moaned at the sensation.

"Lie down."

She was warming to the idea; she was quicker to obey this time.

"Show me."

She parted her lips with one hand and touched the funny little silicone nozzle to her clit with the other. Her face immediately went slack with pleasure, and his cock jerked its approval. He couldn't help himself, his hand squeezed the base and he thrust into his fist.

"Yeah," she moaned.

He wasn't sure if she was moaning in response to the thrum of suction against her clit or the sight of him, but he didn't care a whole lot. It was all the same to his cock.

"Do you—" Her voice was breaking up now, her concentration shot. "Do you do it dry like that?"

It felt like she'd reached out a hand and added her soft stroke to his. He groaned. "I lick my hand sometimes."

"Do it."

He was in the process of lifting his hand to his own mouth when he thought better of it and lowered it to hers. Her tongue came out, flat, wet, rasping against every fingerprint and groove, sending sensation thrilling up his arm. He brought it back to his cock, the strokes slicker now, more like her—and she knew it; a flush was rising in her face.

She did something and the hum of the device working between her legs edged up a notch.

"Did you just turn it up?"

She nodded, wordless.

"Does it feel good?"

"So good."

"God, Auburn."

"Not as good as when you lick me, though," she said, almost conversationally, and he almost lost it.

"But I can't watch you like this when I do that," he said.

"No, you can't."

Her nipples were sharp points. He reached out his spare hand and stroked one, then the other.

"If you keep doing that I'm going to come," she said.

"Yeah," he said. "That's what I want."

"You, too," she said.

"Yeah. Me too."

He was. He was so close that each stroke felt dangerous in the best possible way.

He stopped stroking himself long enough to reach between her legs. She was swollen and soaking, and he covered his fingers in it and brought them back to his cock. He was close, his balls drawn up, his cock so big it felt like it was splitting the skin. Her eyes were riveted on the shiny skin over the head, on the drops of pre-cum forming there.

He hit the point of no return suddenly, the orgasm shooting

up his spine, the pressure in his balls and tension in his limbs all releasing at once with white-hot pleasure. He came hard, all over her soft belly, and she watched the first thick white strand fall on her skin.

That was enough for her, apparently.

"Oh!" she said breathlessly, and her head thrashed from side to side on the pillow, her body bucking, as she came. She was unbelievably beautiful like that, all pleasure and abandon, his cum all over her stomach.

He cleaned them both up with a warm washcloth and lay down beside her, drawing her close against him. Breathing in lavender and the sea-scent of sex.

"Good little device you've got there."

"I don't remember it working that fast or making me come that hard the last time I used it."

He chuckled and kissed her forehead. She snuggled closer.

And that was the last thing he remembered until morning.

33

Trey Xavier was eating pancakes.

And not just eating them, but consuming them with gusto, alternating bites of syrup-drenched hotcake with crispy bacon and fresh local berries. *And* his phone was nowhere to be seen.

She'd awakened around one a.m. with his arm thrown over her. In sleep, in the moonlight streaming in through the window, he'd looked as vulnerable as a little boy. His lashes trembled against his cheeks and his face was relaxed and guileless. He looked nothing like the man she'd first seen in Bob's Tavern, and she'd been overwhelmed by tenderness. She'd curled against him and fallen back asleep.

This morning she'd woken with a whole different set of emotions. In the dark room in the pre-dawn, she remembered the claustrophobia of Patrick's world and the terror of realizing she'd completely lost herself.

Hadn't she promised herself she wouldn't do this? Mix money, sex, and power? Let herself catch feelings for someone before she'd established herself—sister, friend, owner of Beachcrest?

She hastily dressed and slunk back to her room to change. A hot shower and her own clothes, the sun beginning to cast gold through the Beachcrest breakfast room windows, restored her somewhat. In the daylight, the memories and sensations of last night were more vivid and compelling than the awfulness of her old mistake.

She wasn't the woman who'd lost herself.

Trey wasn't Patrick.

As if in answer to this thought, Trey looked up from his giant stack of pancakes and beamed in her direction. He raised an eyebrow in a way that made her body instantly recall the touch of his mouth and crave it again. She bit her lip, and his smile vanished and his eyes went dark.

Maybe they should go on a beach hike today to that secret cove—the one no one was ever at—and take a picnic and a blanket—?

For a moment, she let herself imagine that this might be her life. Trying to decide what delight of the Oregon coast to show Trey next.

But there was no point in thinking about that, was there? About a time when Beachcrest was hers and his company had been saved, and *maybe* he would occasionally make a jaunt up to Tierney Bay to see Carl and Brynn and the boys?

Because what if it *didn't* play out that way?

What if she weren't running Beachcrest and he didn't have his company in San Francisco?

Both those things were still real possibilities.

And she couldn't imagine this—whatever it was between them—outlasting either of those defeats.

It was Friday, not a bank holiday, and in all probability she would hear back from Diane Cooper today. She'd checked the Bootstrapper this morning, and while James's strategies had clearly kicked up the action a few notches—and all four of the romance writers and her siblings had made generous donations —at their current rate it would take them far past Monday to raise even half the money she needed.

If she couldn't get the money, then one of them would lose the thing that mattered most to them.

Trey was sandwiched between the fishermen and the romance writers, entertaining them all with a story about the time, back when he'd been flipping houses and working as a contractor, when he'd accidentally built a front porch on the wrong house.

"And the owner—the husband—comes home from work and I'm almost done, and he comes storming up, yelling, 'What are you *doing*?'" and in my head, I'm like, what? I did exactly what we agreed on. And finally, it becomes clear what's happened, and—so, obviously, I agree to not charge them for the work I've done, or the materials. I mean, they're going to get this front porch for free. And if I do say so myself, it's a beautiful front porch. Big and broad, with plenty of room for furniture, and perfectly situated in a nice spacious front yard—probably going to add fifteen-K in curb appeal to the value of this cute little suburban house—and he says, 'Take it down.'"

"No!" gasps Aria. "Oh, my God, I would *kill* for a front porch. I would sell my soul for one. If I were him, I would have thought I won the lottery."

There was a murmur of yes from the romance writers and even Dewann was nodding his agreement.

"Well, not him. And no matter what I did, I couldn't convince him that he should keep it. I hoped that when his wife got home, she'd talk some sense into him, but no, she was even more pissed than he was about the whole thing. By the end they were both talking about suing me for disrupting the integrity of the house, or something like that, making me promise that I'd restore everything to exactly how it had been, putty up any holes I'd made, all that. So I spent the whole next day unbuilding it. *Two days* lost work. But it taught me a really good lesson. After that, I was like a surgeon: 'Mark yourself with permanent marker before I cut.' 'You're sure you want a porch. Right here? On the front of your house? Here's a sharpie, make an X where you want it. And then sign in blood, please.'"

Auburn watched him, watched him demolish her pancakes and bacon and fruit, watched him make the guests smile, watched *him* smile, and wondered until she couldn't wonder any more.

As the other diners started to drift away, she sat down next to him.

"Hey," he said.

"Hey."

His eyes moved over her face, soft and admiring. It made her warm.

"Trey?"

"What?"

She wanted to ask him what would happen if she couldn't get the money. She knew how it would affect Beachcrest and Home Base, but she wanted to know what it would mean for *them*. But he dug his fork back into his pancakes and crammed a mouthful in and followed it with a slice of bacon and a swig of orange juice. When he'd finished chewing, he grinned at her. "There isn't any more bacon is there? Worked up an appetite yesterday. Must have been the three-legged race."

And she couldn't make herself ask. Sometimes you didn't want to know the answer. Instead she said, "There's this secret beach."

"Is there?" he asked mildly, but his eyes darkened.

"It's usually deserted."

"*Is* it?"

"Unless you have work to do?"

He leaned close, his breath a whisper against her ear.

"The only work I have to do today," he murmured, "is the kind it takes to get you to scream my name."

34

It was technically a woods hike, not a beach hike. They walked several miles, mostly along the ridge of a cliff that rode the edge of the Pacific, the world falling away to one side of them into the vastness of gray water and sky. It wasn't sunny, but Auburn said that was for the best, because then they wouldn't get sunburned on the beach. She said it suggestively, and he thought about the prettiest, pinkest parts of her, exposed to the air and the breeze, which would tease over her nipples and ruffle her curls and—

He was walking behind her and she was wearing a sporty sundress, made of some stretchy material that clung to every curve and flared out into a skirt that didn't even make it to midthigh.

"It's hard to walk with an erection," he said grumpily.

She stopped abruptly and he crashed into her. She turned around.

"I can help with that."

The breath went out of him at the same time the blood plummeted south. "It wasn't meant to be a hint—"

But he didn't even get the whole sentence out before she grabbed his hand and tugged him a short distance off the path and into a secluded grove. Then she was on her knees, grappling with the button and zipper of his cargo shorts, releasing him from his boxers so he sprang up, long and thick. It was a relief to feel the cool air on his hot, tight flesh.

He got to watch her face when she first saw him, too. Eyes big and pupils already blown black, nearly blocking out the last ring of blue. She licked her lips, and not for show, he didn't think. Just because she liked the slickness all over his plump head. Then she was licking him, popping him past the rim of her lips, sucking generously and loudly, which—holy fuck, he would *never* have predicted how much that would turn him on, the sound of her wet mouth. The feel of her tongue, licking stripes up the length of him and swirls around the head.

Some women hated giving blowjobs and some women liked it. Some were decent at it, some weren't. She was so good and so enthusiastic that he was losing his mind. She was finding spots on his cock he hadn't known were there, drawing lines and connecting dots and his balls pulled up so fast, the heat shooting down his spine so he barely had time to warn her, "Jesus, Auburn, I'm going to—"

But she knew. She'd grabbed his ass the moment he'd swelled in her mouth, and she wasn't going to let him go. He came just the way she'd wanted, against the hot, wet back of her throat, so much pleasure he didn't mind losing control.

The truth was, he didn't mind losing control when it came to her.

He leaned back against a tree, trying to catch his breath and get his bearings. His knees were water. "Holy *shit*, Auburn."

She grinned at him. "Better?"

He tipped his head back. "It's hard to walk when you're a

limp rag," he said, but he couldn't make it sound grumpy, not even to joke around with her. He just felt too good.

"There's no pleasing some people," she teased.

It took a while before he could pull himself together, but they made their way along the rest of the main trail and down the nearly invisible, unmarked spur to the secret beach. They came down a series of heavily overgrown switchbacks and stepped off a driftwood snag onto the beach.

"Oh. Wow," he said.

"Pretty, right?"

It was a white sand beach tucked into a cove, cupped on one side by red cliffs and on the other by hillside ruffed with overgrown green. Along the back edge of the beach were boulders, tumbled probably over thousands of years from the cliff above —some smooth, some ragged, gray, brown, reddish, flecked. He leaned against one and stared out at the water, gray like the sky and capped in places with white. "It's amazing."

She took off her running shoes and socks, and he watched as she walked down onto the sand. He knelt and began untying his shoes.

She slung the backpack off her shoulder and began unpacking things from it, then said, suddenly, "Shit."

"What?"

"I forgot—how could I—how could I forget a blanket?"

"We can sit on that rock over there." He gestured.

"But—" She raised her eyebrows.

"Oh. That. Well. Where there's a will, there's a way. And I *definitely* have the will."

She laughed at that. "Me too."

He kissed her. "Mmm. Lots of will."

"You just— are you always ready to go?"

"Pretty much," he admitted.

"Not that I mind. At all."

"I didn't get the feeling you did."

He stepped close to her, put a hand on each thigh, and slowly, slowly, slid the stretchy fabric of her dress upward until it revealed a peek of sun-yellow all-lace shorts-style undies. The dark thatch of her mound showed through clearly, and his body bucked at the sight.

"This wrecks me," he said. He edged closer, giving her a feel of what she did to him, and she chuckled against his shoulder.

"It's all yours."

"No one's going to come down—?"

She shrugged. "Hope not. Don't care."

That was even better than *no*. He wasn't an exhibitionist, but the faint possibility of getting caught ... he didn't hate the thrill that added to the already sharp brilliance of his arousal.

"See that rock?"

She went, with a coy backward look over her shoulder that made him want to sink his teeth into something.

He was already unfastening his shorts (again) as he came close to where she leaned against the smooth gray surface.

"Touch yourself."

She watched him from under lowered eyelids as she slid her hand between lace and curls, parted herself, and began a slow circling that he could feel tightening in his balls.

"Are you wet?"

"So wet," she said.

"I can see how hard your nipples are."

She moaned.

He slid a hand up her ribs until his hand met resistance.

"Sorry—built-in sports bra—here—" She showed him how to slide a hand under the elastic, and the weight of her breast in his palm made him twice as hard.

He went to work on the nub that was still stiffening against the touch of his palm. "Does it feel good?"

"So good," she said, her head falling back.

With the other hand, he dipped and tested for himself. She was soft and slick and his patience—not that he'd had much to begin with—flew away. He eased two fingers into her and found her g-spot, stroking until she gasped. Then he slipped a condom from his pocket, stripped the wrapper off, and covered himself.

35

He lifted her like she weighed nothing. For a moment she thought he was going to press her back against the rock, brace her there, but he eyed it gravely and said, "That's going to scrape up your back. I've got you."

He did, one hand under her butt, the other splayed across her back, so she wrapped her hand around him—eliciting a groan—and guided him into her as he lifted her up. The downstroke was long and blissful. It felt like forever before he was fully seated, and then he felt deeper than he had yet. Like he was touching some part of her no one had.

She put her hands on his shoulders, closed her eyes, and let him rock her up and down. The sensation quickly concentrated itself where the weight of her body met the base of his cock. On top of the perfect friction on her clit, he felt bigger in this position, like he was stretching her to the absolute limit, and her whole body responded by trying to clench back around him.

She was going to come in record time, and he knew it. She wasn't sure if he saw it in her eyes or felt the telltale flutters and contractions, but the hand on her behind tightened and lifted her, and he held his hips back from her. "Not yet."

"Trey."

"I know, baby. I know it feels good. But not yet. You feel too good to me. I don't want it to be over."

He took a slow pace, now, giving her most but not all of him, gliding her on her own wetness and turning the whole thing into summery, languid sweetness. Sweat prickled all over her body, in part from the warmth rising off the sand and the heat of his body, but mostly from the loveliness of the sensation. Like sun sparkling on the surface of blue ocean, especially when he angled himself to catch her g-spot with the fat head of his cock. She cried out on every rich, glittery touch. Her body relaxed around him a tiny bit, giving up more moisture, slicking his thrusts, and he groaned with satisfaction. "You're so tight and so wet and smooth at the same time. It's crazy good."

"Your arms must be tired," she whispered hopefully, but he just chuckled and slowed the pace even more. The muscles bunched and flared in his shoulders and chest and arms, setting up new tingles in the few spots where bare skin met bare skin.

"Can I do this?" she asked, and leaned back a little.

"Oh, shit, yeah, you can do that. Oh. That angle. Auburn."

"Me, too," she whispered.

She became aware that the sensation was building again, in a different way from before. From deeper, and without any tension in her muscles.

And he fucking knew, too, the bastard. He stopped. And held her still.

The silvery, glittery sensation didn't stop, though. It kept rippling through her. And it kept building. It didn't need motion. It was feeding on the heat of Trey's skin and the strength of his arms around her and how much she liked him.

"Trey."

"Mmm-hmm."

"I'm going to—oh, fuck! Ohhhhh. Trey! God. More."

He gave it to her, tugging her down, surging into her, filling her, stretching her, so the sparkling bliss of the orgasm blended with the sensation of fullness into a perfect storm.

She could feel his thrusts growing ragged and uneven. Then he swelled in her, cried out, and went rigid, his head thrown back, the cords of his neck standing out. Every muscle was hard against her. It was so goddamn sweet, this big, alpha all-businessman, always so tightly in control of himself and everything else he could get his hands on, breaking *because of her*. It almost made her come again, but there was a little part of her standing apart, watching warily just in case he lost control completely and dropped her.

He didn't, of course. He held her and held her and held her, and she let him, even though she was so, so afraid it couldn't last forever.

AFTERWARDS, they stuffed themselves on picnic food—melon chunks, a pasta salad with basil and tomatoes and lots of freshly grated parmesan cheese, sliced veggies in hummus, and a small charcuterie of cured meats and cheeses. Eating together after what they'd done—it was a certain kind of lovely pleasure—the salt and the sweet and the bonelessness of being relaxed together.

Then they packed up—carefully removing all traces of their presence—and hiked back to the car.

They'd brought Trey's rental—Auburn still hadn't saved up enough to buy a car of her own—and they slid into their seats and both reached simultaneously for their cell phones, which made them laugh. By agreement, they'd left their phones in the car—Luz was at the front desk of Beachcrest, and Carl was resting but on hand to answer questions if there was anything that Luz couldn't handle—generally speaking, though, there wasn't.

He made a small noise of dismay.

"What?"

"Voicemail from my Chief of Ops."

"Is that bad?"

"No. Not bad. Just—I told him I'd call him when I had news for him." He tapped and listened, his face tightening as she watched. Then he tapped to end the call and just sat, staring straight ahead.

"What did he say?"

He looked away from her, out the window.

"Trey?"

"Nothing he hasn't said before. I don't work for him, anyway. He works for me."

"You can tell me."

He took a deep breath. "The crux is that he thinks if you don't have the money by close of business on the West coast today, you should call Carl off."

Her stomach clenched. "I thought we had till Monday."

"He doesn't want to cut it that close. He says nothing's going to happen over the weekend to change the dynamics of the situation. He wants papers signed Monday morning. Wants you to have your argument with Carl over the weekend, not haggling while the purchase and sale is on the table."

"The Bootstrapper—" She watched his face and knew. "You don't think it's going to work."

"I think—I think we might be able to tell by the end of today. If it stands a chance. We can do the math."

"There's still Diane Cooper. The other lender."

He nodded. "Did she call?"

For the first time she looked down at her own phone. And shook her head.

"Not yet."

"Well," he said. "There's still time. It's barely two."

"I should call her. I told her I needed to know quickly, but I should let her know I've got until end of day."

He nodded.

She made the call, got put through to voicemail. Hung up.

"It's not the end of the world ..." she began.

"Don't," he said. "She's going to call back, and she's going to do the loan. It's just good business. Beachcrest is a great investment."

She smiled at that. "I've really won you over, huh?"

He set his phone on the dashboard. Reached out, cupped her cheek in his warm hand. Leaned and kissed her, soft and slick and hungry.

"You could say that."

36

The call came at 4:39. They were dozing on Trey's bed together, boneless and sleepy from their various exertions. He woke fully before she did, grabbed her phone from the nightstand, and thrust it into her hand. He saw her eyes go big and worried; then she took the call with, "Auburn Campbell, speaking."

He watched her face, saw the moment.

"Yes, of course. No, of course—I understand. Any possibility of—even a few percentage points—no, yes, right. Makes sense. Well. Thank you for considering."

She ended the call and sat with the phone held tight in her hand, not moving.

"No loan," he said, just so she wouldn't have to. None of this was her fault. She shouldn't be in this situation. She would never have been in this situation if it hadn't been for him.

"Fifteen percent down is the best she can do," she said. She seemed to wake up then, suddenly snapping to attention and swiping open the phone again. "We should look at the Bootstrapper. And then—well, we should make a call."

He felt like he was standing on the edge of a very high cliff.

She tapped through the app until she brought up what she was looking for. And then she sighed. He felt the sigh to the bottoms of his feet. She handed her phone to him, and he looked. She'd raised fourteen thousand dollars, which was—

"It's not a bad haul," he said feebly.

"But it's not a viral campaign. Or even one that's about to go viral."

"No. No, it's not."

"So—"

"Auburn—"

"Look," she said decisively. "I've been giving this a *lot* of thought. There's really no choice here. I don't have the money. *We* don't have the money."

"I don't have the money."

"It wasn't yours to have," she said.

"But this is happening because of me. Because I made a bad investment. A bad choice. If I'd been a good steward for Home Base, I would never have had to put you in this position. I could have given you weeks or even months to come up with the money. Hell, I could have done a Contract for Deed or even financed the whole purchase for you."

She made a face at that. "What makes you think I would have let you do *that*?" she teased, and for just a moment, the levity in her voice helped. Made him feel like things were going to be okay.

"The point is," she said, "there's no money." She made it carefully neutral, like that might make him forget the circumstances. "And given that fact—I think it's pretty damn obvious that it's time for me to back down. Call off Carl."

"I think we should at least talk about the alternative."

She was shaking her head. "No. Don't even say it, Trey. I know you'll hate yourself if you say it. If it were just you, I *know* you'd do it. You'd do some kind of crazy self-sacrificing grand gesture and give me Beachcrest. But it's not just you. And I know you wouldn't be able to live with yourself if a hundred and fifty people lost their jobs. You're not that kind of man."

"You mean," he said darkly, "you're not that kind of woman." Because right now he had *no* idea what kind of man he was. Not the man who'd gone toe to toe with her in a hospital room, for sure, but not, by a goddamn long shot, the man she deserved. The man he'd set out to be, the kind who would never steal from someone he cared about the thing that mattered most to her. She was going to lose Beachcrest. The woman in front of him was going to lose the place she lived, her livelihood—her *life's dream* because of him.

He was no better than Patrick.

Worse, he was no better than his father.

"There's only one thing to do," she said. "We'll talk to Carl. He'll understand." Her eyes flicked to his face, suddenly seeing, with an understanding so instant and thorough that it almost made him howl with grief, what that was going to mean to him. "Oh," she said. "We'll have to tell him. What—"

"What I did. That I fucked up."

"You made a mistake. People make mistakes all the time in business."

"I got greedy," he said. "I knew that investment was riskier than our usual tolerance, but I thought—"

"You thought if you grew this company big enough to sell that you'd be in a position to make sure Brynn lived in a bigger house and Carl got to retire in comfort," she said. "I know that's what you thought."

And there she was, giving him the benefit of the doubt because that's the kind of person she was, one with a heart so big it could hold everything—all the strays who wandered into Beachcrest, all the world's mistakes, the loss of the thing she'd wanted most.

"I got greedy," he said. "I wasn't thinking about Brynn or Carl. I was thinking about me and my reputation and the next big thing. I was looking ahead instead of focusing on what was in front of me, and now I *should* be paying for it. But—" his chest was so tight that it came out choked. Strangled. "Instead, you're paying for it. Tell me how the fuck that's fair."

"It's *not* fair," Auburn said. "If you think that's what I'm saying, you're way off. But it's also life. Beachcrest was never mine, Trey. I didn't have the money. I never had the money, and that wasn't anything to do with you. It was just the truth of my life. It was crazy, naive, idealistic, for me to think that just because Carl said it would be mine one day that somehow, *magically,* it would."

More than anything, he hated the way she'd just said the word *magically*, as if magic were something she had believed in before but didn't anymore. Something she'd grown out of.

"You know, and I know, that the well-being of all your employees combined has to outweigh just mine," Auburn said.

He couldn't bring himself to agree with her. He just couldn't. The words wouldn't come out of his mouth, wouldn't move past the choke point in his chest.

"Trey."

People didn't always know what they wanted. They wanted to live in a shack when there was a mansion for sale, to retire in a hovel when there was a luxury condo in the offing. They couldn't see that they'd placed their faith in the wrong man, that it was only a matter of time before they'd be worn down to the nub or blown away like dust.

She took both his hands. Hers were warm; he could feel that his were like ice.

"We need to talk to Carl."

She'd been wrong about Patrick and she was wrong about

him, and both times she hadn't been able to see the truth until it was too late.

He saw exactly what he needed to do.

But he didn't say any of it aloud, because he knew she'd fight him. She always fought him—it was one of the things he loved most about her.

Instead he said, "He's at Brynn's right now. We'll talk to him when he gets back."

He'd thought he'd already done the worst thing. He thought he'd ruined everything that was left to ruin. But when she smiled at him and said, "Sounds good," he knew there was one thing left to destroy, and he'd just signed its death warrant.

37

S he went into Beachcrest's tiny office to put things in order. Trey had said that the closing would have to be within the next thirty days, which meant that she'd have to cancel all the reservations from August 1 on. The thought made her stomach hurt, badly—and tears filled her eyes—especially when she thought about the Gardners, who always came in September and had for more than ten years, to celebrate their wedding anniversary. And the Hoopers in October, and Carson and Sage and their families at Christmas ... and on and on. But this was how it was; they had done their best, and it hurt, but it was life.

She was still sitting in there, an hour and a half later, when she heard Trey's voice, just a murmur on the other side of her closed door. Talking to Luz.

She came out of the office. "Hey!" she said. She was determined to be upbeat; what was happening was awful; it was impossible to think about without misery, but she wouldn't wallow and she wouldn't guilt-trip Trey.

Luz looked from her to Trey, then bit her lip. "I'm going to go check on the kitchen inventory," she said, slipping between them and out to the back of the inn. "Auburn can help you with whatever you need help with."

She and Trey were alone at the front desk, facing each other, once again, over its width.

The grave expression on his face made anxiety skitter across the floor of her stomach. But she took a deep breath. She'd known getting past this would be weird and hard, but they were good. They had to be good. What had passed between them during the last few days had to mean something to him, as it did to her; she *knew* it. You couldn't just walk away from that kind of chemistry.

"Is Carl back?"

"He's still at Brynn's, but—it's good. I took care of it. I explained it all to him. He was angry I hadn't told him any of it before. He's just plain angry. He called me a lot of things I probably deserved—"

It took her brain a minute to catch up to him. "You talked to Carl. Without me... That wasn't the deal we made earlier, Trey."

"I know. But I didn't want to put you through that. It's not your mess to clean up."

"You said we'd talk to him when he came back from Brynn's! And then, what, as soon as I wasn't looking, you drove over there? Which means, you lied to me, doesn't it?"

The expression on his face answered the question.

"Because I knew you'd try to tell him this wasn't my fault—"

"Well, yeah! I would tell him how I saw things. That's why I wanted to talk to him with you, so we could make him see the big picture—" Then she caught her breath, realizing she was missing the more important point. "What happened isn't your fault, Trey."

"Yeah," he said. "Yeah, it fucking is. There's no version of the universe in which it's not my fault. I made the decisions that put Home Base where it was. I made the choices that brought me here. And then I put you in an impossible position and forced you to make an untenable decision. And—" He took a deep breath; she heard it catch somewhere in his chest. "I need to own that, Auburn."

"People make bad business decisions, Trey. They make mistakes. They don't think things all the way through. And sometimes there are unintended consequences. I don't blame you for any of that."

"You should," he said. "I blame myself. I can't forgive myself for letting this happen."

She was starting to get a very bad feeling about this. "So—so what does that mean?"

He took a deep breath and looked away, his gaze roaming the corners of the room before landing back on her face. "I'm going back to San Francisco."

"For how long?"

As soon as the words left her mouth, as soon as his expression shifted, a curtain falling behind his eyes, she knew. But he said it anyway. "For good."

"When you say 'for good,' what exactly do you mean?"

She was surprised—and pleased—to hear her voice sound almost normal. Like she was just asking a casual question. Not one that was forced up from her soul, even though that was what it felt like.

He shook his head. "I don't think we should see each other again."

He reached out and set something on the shiny surface of the front desk, pushed it across to her. It was the key to his room.

For a moment, she could only stare at it. Then her mind clicked back into motion. "You. Don't. Think." She stopped. "*You* don't think we should see each other again. And just like that—" She snapped her fingers. "That's it. None of that happened."

"Auburn, this isn't about *you*."

"No?" she asked, arching an eyebrow. "Please, do explain. Explain how this isn't about me. Because I'm not seeing it. I'm feeling like this is about me in every possible way. Because *I* am the one who just lost the place I live and work and love. *I* am the one who spent this last week trying my damnedest to make everything work out for Beachcrest, and for me, and *fuck it,* for *you,* Trey! *I* am the one who was there when you talked about your childhood and your failed marriage and your over-leveraged business, when you ate biscuits and bacon and marshmallows, when we danced and raced and when you—" Words failed her; the images of him moving over her and inside her, watching her shatter, spilling as she watched him, were too much for words. "So, how exactly is this not about me?"

"It's about me." He sounded agonized. "And what I can't give you. I can't take care of you. I didn't take care of you. I don't deserve you."

"Oh, my *God,* is that really how you see this? That this is all about you and what you did? Do you have *any idea* what an asshole that makes you?"

It was funny that of all the things he'd done, this was the one that finally, finally made her angry. Because he'd done it *to* her, after everything that had happened between them, knowing how she felt about having her autonomy taken away from her. "So you just decide to write me out. Make this your story, tell it like you see it, decide what you need to do about it, and not even take me into account."

"I *am* taking you into account. You deserve someone who can take care of you."

"I *deserve* someone who treats me like a human being with free will. I *deserve* someone who doesn't make decisions that definitely are *about* me ... *for* me!"

She was shouting. It took a lot to make her shout. She'd

never shouted at Patrick. She'd never really even gotten mad at him. She'd let Chiara do it for her.

Maybe that had been a mistake. Because it felt pretty good to let someone have it.

"*I* helped make this decision. We were working together to solve a problem, and we made a deal! You don't get to storm out of the room if you don't like the terms you get. You don't get to ruin all the good that's come out of this week because you have to be the big man on campus."

"What good has come out of this week?" he demanded. "At the end of the week, you have nothing. No place to live. No place to work. No future."

"What *good* has come out of this week?" she echoed. "Where *were* you? Did you not have the same week I had? Because all I *saw* was good. I saw you laugh and relax and make friends, and that sure as hell wasn't happening last week. I saw you—I saw lots and lots of people—enjoying the beach and campfires and marshmallows and parades and barbecues and family. I saw people spending time together who hadn't been together for too long. My first July 4th with my family in years. Also, I had some really fucking great sex. But apparently, you were just waiting to see how it would all *end*, and if it didn't end the way you wanted it to, you would just write the whole fucking thing off, like the control freak you are. Well fuck you, Xavier. *Fuck you.* And just in case it matters, I fucking *love* you."

If she'd expected that to work like some extreme magic spell, she was sorely disappointed. His expression barely changed.

"That doesn't mean anything if you can't take care of the person you love."

"I. Don't. Need. You. To. Take. Care. Of. Me. And neither does Brynn and neither does Carl. Maybe you need to take care of us or else you feel like an epic failure—but that's *your* problem, now, isn't it?"

Her chest was heaving like she'd run a mile. Or like it had every time he'd gotten close enough to touch her. She tried to catch her breath, but it was a lost cause; she was too angry, she was too hurt—*how had she been such an idiot?*

Again.

"Go," she said. "Just, go. Go take care of all the people who work for you whose asses you just saved and enjoy feeling like a big damn hero. You want to go back to San Francisco? Fine." She grabbed the key from the counter, yanked open the drawer, dropped the key in, and slammed it shut.

"You're checked out."

38

"I brought molten chocolate cake from the Tierney Bay Diner."

Chiara set the boxes down on the night table next to Auburn's bed.

"You're a saint," Auburn said.

"Hardly. Just a sister."

"A good sister."

Chiara opened the two boxes. Each held a single dark round of tender lava cake and a scoop of vanilla ice cream. She stuck a spoon into each and pushed one toward Auburn.

Auburn took a bite, gave a small sigh of satisfaction and despair, and slumped back against the headboard.

"You said chocolate. And ice cream. This was the purest hit I could score."

Auburn sat up, took another spoonful. The soft chocolate melted on her tongue, and the contrast between the hot of the cake and the cold of the ice cream took her out of her own misery for the first time that day.

"So. Are you going to tell me what happened?"

She did. How the other financing option had fallen through.

How the Bootstrapper, even with James's help and all the advertising support, hadn't moved the needle. How she and Trey had looked down into the mouth of the cannon and made the best call they could.

"It's over," she told her sister. "We did everything we could, but it wasn't enough to save Beachcrest. Or each other."

And there it was—she burst into tears. Ugly, snotty tears. But Chiara, being Chiara, didn't care, just found the box of tissues in the bathroom and passed them, one by one, to Auburn, until she could talk again.

"You didn't tell me how the breakup went down."

"No. I didn't."

So she told that part, too. His high-handedness, his arrogance, his insistence on doing it his way, telling his story to Carl, icing her out, deciding their fate without her, seeing the whole thing through the lens of his actions. And when she was done, she said, "I wish—I wish I'd stuck to my guns. I knew as soon as I smelled that fucking cologne. A zebra doesn't change its Armani stripes. Not every guy in a suit is Patrick, but every asshole who dons a suit, even if he's willing to wear beach clothes for a few days to get what he wants, is *still* an asshole."

She went through a few more tissues then, because she was so angry at herself for doing it again. Sex, money, power.

"If you want, Mason and Levi could probably have him killed," Chiara said.

That made Auburn smile through her tears. "They're pretty self-sufficient; they'd probably do it themselves. But no. I think it's too late for that. Wish I'd thought of it earlier this week." She snickered, then sobered up. "Truly, I think the Beachcrest sale was always inevitable. But acting like a self-righteous douche bag? He did that." She crossed her arms. "It probably doesn't deserve death. Just an ice cold ghosting."

"Sounds like a plan," Chiara said. She tilted her head, indicating Auburn's now dormant dessert, melting into a big mess. "The romance writers are playing Pandemic in the dining room —want to go join them?"

"I couldn't even save Beachcrest; how am I supposed to save the world?"

"You saved a hundred and fifty jobs."

"And lost Luz's and Sarah's and mine. And Carl's legacy."

"I'm sorry, Auburn. I'm so sorry. But Levi's still hiring, so Luz and Sarah will be fine. And you'll be fine too. If you don't want to work for Levi—"

"I don't think Cape House needs two managers."

"Me neither." Chiara sighed. "At least you're in the right part of the world to find another position."

Auburn smiled, an effort, but it felt good to do it. "I'm going to give myself just a little while to feel sorry for myself, and then I'll get back on my feet. I've done it before—" More times than she wanted to think about, but she was good at it. "And I'll do it again. The truth is, it's just a building. It's not actually an enchanted castle in a fairytale."

Chiara looked stricken at that, but Auburn just shook her head. "There's no such a thing as magic, in the end. I'll start again somewhere. Abracadabra, new life."

She took a last bite of the molten cake and ice cream soup— she'd hit that stage of eating where the taste had gone out and she was just spooning it into her mouth reflexively—and said, "You know what, let's go play Pandemic. Feels like the end of the world, so why not?"

"Are you sure?"

"Positive."

"Asia's a mess. Look," Priya said, indicating the heaps of red cubes on the Pandemic game board. "We spent too much time trying to cure and not enough time trying to treat."

"We don't have the medic card this time, which was a bad move," Lindsey said.

"Where's your hot billionaire?" Aria demanded. "Get him. If I'm going to lose this stupid game and decimate the world's population, I should have something pretty to look at while I do it."

Chiara and Auburn exchanged glances.

"He left," Auburn said.

"What?!" A chorus of romance writers.

She sat down and brought them up to date on the events of the day.

"Well, shoot!" Aria said. "We were going to come back at Christmas and next summer. We were going to make it our place!"

A glum mood settled over the six of them, and they gazed down at the board. Auburn could still feel Deja's gaze on her. "I'm so sorry, baby," the older woman said.

"It's okay."

"No. It's not. We led you wrong."

Auburn brushed it off with firm sweep of her hand. "It was a rock and a hard place from the beginning. You tried to squeeze me through a tunnel that turned out to narrow to a crevice."

"You ever think about writing books?"

Auburn grinned and shook her head.

"You got a gift for a turn of phrase."

"Not like you."

"It's not just Beachcrest that's got you down, is it? It's *him*."

Auburn sighed. "He had a heart of gold, but it's buried too deep underground."

Deja smiled at that. "Common problem with hot billionaires," she said dryly. "Only way to fix them is to keep digging, even if you need to use a pickax. Literally."

"I don't think you mean literally," Lindsey whispered.

"Oh, I do," Deja murmured back.

Auburn couldn't help a small smile. "Yeah, well. I don't want to keep digging. I don't want to be with a guy like that."

"You could tell him not to talk and to just give up the goods," Aria said.

"That came out of your mouth," Deja told her friend.

"Gah. Sorry."

"We need to get this woman some ice cream. Or chocolate," Priya declared.

"Already done that," Chiara said. "This is not our first rodeo."

"Rodeo," Aria mused. "Do you think you could do hot billionaire at the rodeo?"

"With amnesia," Priya put in.

"Head injury. From falling off. Doesn't remember he's rich. Falls for ... oh, my goodness gracious, Auburn, take over my seat, I have to go write this down.

Auburn surveyed the mess that was the map of the world.

"Can't keep Beachcrest from being torn down," she said. "Can't seem to stop making the same dumbass romantic mistakes. But fuck me if I can't save the world from the rampages of biowarfare."

39

In the morning she made waffles.

She'd had the flu late last fall in New York, right before she'd left Patrick. She hadn't been able to get out of bed because her body ached like it had been hit by a truck and she got nauseated if she stood up. Patrick had been busy making a deal, but he'd had his housekeeper care for Auburn, bringing her chicken soup and orange juice and echinacea. After a week she'd been able to rise for short periods of time, but she'd felt like she was moving underwater, suffocated and weighed down, the world strangely sluggish and bland.

That was how she felt this morning. She watched her arm move, beating the batter in the bowl, but she felt strangely disconnected from it. She carried plates out and set them down in front of her guests; she smiled at them and made conversation, but she couldn't have told you what anyone said.

When she'd left Patrick, she'd felt liberated. Terrified, yes. But elated.

Right now? She felt like a mug that had been shattered and glued back together again.

"What should we do today?" Priya asked.

"Have you been to Nehalem Bay State Park?"

Priya shook her head.

"It's really pretty. And the weather's nice, so you could have a real beach day. There are horseback rides down there, too."

"Research," Aria said. "For my cowboy."

"This stay has been so inspiring," Priya said. "I don't think I've ever done a writing retreat where there's been so much material to draw on." And then she fell silent, her gaze dropping to the table, realizing what she'd said, and how it didn't matter anymore.

Auburn's own chest felt painfully tight, but it wasn't the flu.

When most of the others had gone, Dewann and Rick were left. It was their morning to check out, and they'd already brought their suitcases down and stowed them behind the front desk.

"So," Auburn said, as she picked up their plates. "When will you two be back in Tierney Bay?"

She hadn't made a general announcement to her guests about what was going to happen to Beachcrest. She'd wait until —well, until the documents were signed, she guessed.

Dewann and Rick exchanged glances. "Well, funny you should ask. We, er, bought a place."

"You—"

"A little house. A shack, really. Out a ways, just off 101. So we won't be coming to Beachcrest anymore. Because, well, we'll live here."

"Together," Rick said.

Auburn didn't let her surprise or pleasure show. If she made a big fuss, she'd embarrass them both. She just said, "Well, congratulations, then."

She was about to say, *Would you still come have breakfast for old time's sakes?* And then she remembered. It kept slipping away and surging back, the realization that it was all ending, that there would be no more Beachcrest breakfasts, or anything else. No old time's sakes. No memories to revisit, no people coming back to hold weddings after they'd met here, or to commemorate anniversaries after they'd married here. No one renewing vows for 60ths after celebrating 10ths.

Not ever.

And the weight of it threatened for a moment to crush her.

Then she saw the way Dewann was looking at Rick, and Rick was looking back at Dewann. It was pure joy and devotion in their eyes—a kind of peace and acceptance and *freedom* that she hadn't seen very many times on their faces.

And everything shifted, like a spell had been lifted.

Or cast, maybe. Like some magic had been done.

She took a deep breath for what felt like the first time in days.

"It's not just about me, is it?"

"What isn't?" Rick asked, understandably confused.

"Beachcrest. Keeping it. Selling it."

Dewann tilted his head, listening patiently.

"It's about you guys. And Carl. And Deja and the others ... Priya saying this was the best place to have a writing retreat."

And Trey, she thought, but didn't say it aloud. She wasn't even a hundred percent sure what she meant by including him. Only that—well, if there had ever been a person who needed Beachcrest, it was Trey Xavier. She hoped—

She hoped that he would still laugh sometimes and eat the occasional biscuit or hot dog. And maybe he would think about her when he did.

Even though she was still angry at him and hurt. For being so stubborn and not having faith that she could take care of herself and know what she wanted ...

And for ruining what they had.

She was so, so angry at him for that.

But that wasn't the point. The point was—

The point was that she couldn't just give up. She'd thought she could, but she couldn't. She couldn't because Beachcrest belonged to her, and to Dewann and to Rick and to Carl and to Deja and Aria and Priya and Lindsey and to everyone who had ever come to stay there. To Trey. So even if it looked impossible, even if time had run out and Trey and Doug and everyone else had given up, she had to try to save it.

For them.

She took a deep breath.

"I have an idea."

40

"You okay, man?"

It was Monday, *the* Monday, early afternoon, and the voice was Doug's. Trey lifted his head from where it rested in his hands, his elbows on the wide oak of his ridiculously over-the-top desk, and looked into the eyes of his chief operating officer.

"Sure," Trey lied.

It had been jarring, the switch back to his own life.

Sitting in traffic on the way from the airport to Home Base's offices, his phone in his hand, he was aware of the last of the languor slipping from his limbs. At some point, without his noticing, the freeways and roads of San Francisco had become crowded and hostile, Uber drivers darting into and out of traffic, his own driver cursing grumpily. Every email bumping his adrenaline up. His brain didn't want to do it; didn't want to shift from one mode—the warmth and generosity of Auburn's existence—to another—his, amped up and barren.

He'd been sitting at his desk all morning, waiting to feel like his work mattered, but mostly he'd thought about how it felt to have sand between his toes, the heat of a beach fire on his face,

Auburn's body wrapped around his in all the possible ways, losing himself completely in the sensation of it.

"I've got the purchase and sale for you to sign," Doug said.

Although he'd been waiting all day for this moment—the moment that had been approaching with the inevitability of a head-on collision, for hours—he still felt the painful drop of lead in his gut.

Doug laid the document—a sheaf of white decorated with fluorescent sticky-note flags—on the desk in front of Trey.

He leafed through it, but the words blurred and wriggled. He was just turning pages, not making any sense out of what he saw. "You looked at it? Legal looked at it? It's in order?"

Doug nodded. "They've signed. Carl's signed. All you need to do is sign where it's flagged."

"And then it's done. Beachcrest is gone, Home Base is saved."

"Then it's done."

He found the first line awaiting his signature. Opened his pen, set the tip of the pen to the page. Signed.

But when he came to the second, he set the pen back down on the desk, closed his eyes, and rested his head in his hands again.

"You want to tell me about her?" Doug asked quietly.

"Who?" Trey looked up.

"Who do you think, Xavier? The woman who's making you consider throwing all this away." Doug gestured around them, and Trey obediently looked, but couldn't make sense of 'all this.' All *what*? The posturing furniture? The money whose purpose was to mint more money? Building and building and building, one block on another—for what? Like a kid who tried to build a tower to reach the moon? "She must be something."

"She—"

He could still see her face, so angry, so hurt.

"I ruined her *life*."

"If her personal happiness hinged on a hotel that didn't belong to her, she sort of had it coming."

Anger rose up in him, hot and fierce. "She didn't deserve any of this. Not one little bit. She's too good for this kind of bullshit. And I could have been honest with her from the beginning, I could have told her there was no way this could work out—instead I played a game with her—to get what I wanted. To keep from losing money *so I could make more money.*"

"That's what you do, Trey. You make money. And then you make more money. For your stakeholders. For your investors. For your employees. That's your *job*. And speaking of your job, once you get this thing signed, let's talk about what we're going to do next. I want in, whatever it is."

"Even though I almost blew this."

"You always had it in hand."

It was the exact opposite of the truth. From the moment he'd seen Auburn Campbell in Bob's Tavern, he'd *never* had it in hand. It had been completely and totally out of his control and he'd been profoundly and thoroughly out of his depth—

Yet it had been, quite possibly, the best week of his life.

"Yes. I want to work with you on whatever you do next. I'm thinking something else in the same space. More real estate tech. Or health care tech, although I feel like that's more tapped out. Or—I'm willing to look at block chain if you are. This time I want in, though, from the ground floor."

"You can be in for whatever you've got," Trey said.

"Excellent. So. Sign this fucker and we'll get on with it. Make you a billionaire next time, right? Unicorn status. Put you on the map. Get your name in those 'biggest deals of' or 'highest valuation' lists. Just pick up the goddamn pen, man. Pull yourself together and pick up the goddamn pen."

He did. He opened it. Set the tip on the page and signed again.

"Two down. Forty-seven more to go," Doug said.

"Are there really that many signatures?"

"No. Keep fucking signing."

On the desk, Trey's phone began to buzz. Instinctively, he reached for it.

The number was unfamiliar but the name he'd attached it to made his whole body buzz at the same frequency as the device.

Auburn.

"Don't get that," Doug said. "Finish signing."

He almost obeyed. Because there was no point, because this was where they were now. This was what had to be done, and anything that chipped away at his resolve would only make life more difficult for all of them.

It quit ringing, and he exhaled and signed the third line.

And then it started again.

Auburn.

He picked it up and answered. "Xavier speaking."

He heard her intake of breath and then she said, "I want to make an offer for Beachcrest."

41

She'd handed the phone off to her lawyer, right away, even though he'd said, "Wait—"

The lawyer named the number, then began making a case for why Trey should accept the offer, but Trey cut him off.

"I accept."

"You accept *what*?" Doug demanded.

"Auburn's buying Beachcrest."

"No," Doug said. "Royal Life is going to fucking *kill* me. They're never going to do business with us again."

"I don't care," Trey said.

"Excuse me?" the lawyer asked.

"Sorry," Trey said.

"You need to think about this for a minute," Doug said.

"I don't," Trey said, and then, "Sorry," again, to the lawyer. "I don't suppose you could tell me where she got the money for the down payment—"

The lawyer made a sharp noise of disgust.

"No, I suppose you really can't," Trey concluded for himself.

He didn't care. He shouldn't care. Even if it was Patrick who'd given her the money, he had no *right* to care.

He told the lawyer to fax over the P&S. He talked Doug off the ledge, and got him, still miffed but understanding that there was zero chance he'd change Trey's mind, out of his office. And then he was on Beachcrest's Facebook page, digging for a post, any post, that would fill in the missing pieces.

How the *hell* had she come up with hundreds of thousands of dollars over the weekend?

He found the digital trail without too much trouble. And the whole idea was sheer brilliance. Of course it was. Of course she'd figured it out. He couldn't believe he'd ever doubted her.

In the end, she'd done it as a Bootstrapper campaign, after all. A series of incentives, the granddaddy of which was an all-expenses paid weekend-long "experience weekend" with the romance writers. Romance campfires, beach bike rides, cookies and tea, signed books, goody baskets full of swag, writing lessons and workshops. And he could see from the trail of shares leading in both directions that Deja, Aria, Lindsey, and Priya had each placed several Facebook ads and pimped the getaway to all their readers, that it had gone viral in the romance community. There were thousands of comments on the Facebook posts, and nearly that many contributions on the Bootstrapper page. She had enough for a down payment *and* she'd be able to do a kitchen renovation.

He hadn't ruined everything. Something good had come out of her association with him, after all. She'd been able to turn their week together into the thing that had saved Beachcrest for her. And—more to the point—on her own terms. All he was going to do, in the end, was sign the closing documents with (a very willing) Carl.

Technically he didn't have to go back to Tierney Bay to do that. He could sign the deal from San Fran. But Brynn's garage door was acting up, and Carl was still not supposed to lift anything heavy, so on Tuesday he flew back to Tierney Bay and helped Brynn replace one of the big springs in the garage door mechanism, trying not to injure either himself or his curious nephews in the process.

Brynn, of course, only wanted to talk about Beachcrest and Auburn.

"It was really clever, what she did, wasn't it?"

Genius, really, but he just grunted a yes, his attention focused on the spring.

"You can pretend you don't care, but I know you do," Brynn said.

At that, he put his tools down and turned to her. On her, really. "What do you want from me?"

Like a chain reaction, Brynn rounded on her boys, who were listening to the adult conversation with the rapt attention of small people who have no idea what's being said, only that it might contain a germ of scandal. "Go. Go—have some screen time."

Their eyes got enormous at the sudden boon.

"Quick! Before I change my mind!"

They ran.

Trey felt twice as exposed with them gone. Like they'd been the only thing protecting him from his sister's wrath.

Or maybe the truth.

Brynn pushed a finger toward his chest. "I want you to admit that you care for her. That you love her. No," she said. "I want you to tell *her* that you love her. That you're miserable without her. That you want her back."

"She's better off without me. And I'm better off without her."

"Neither of those things is true. I saw you guys together. I saw how you were with her. You're both better together."

He shrugged, because it made his chest hurt less. "She definitely didn't think so. She called me an asshole and a control freak and told me to go away and not come back. And she has a point. What makes me better than her ex?"

"The fact that you love her and want to do right by her?"

"Don't you think he thought he did?"

"Trey," Brynn said quietly.

"Don't. Please, don't."

"Someone needs to, dude. Someone needs to tell you you're being—"

She hesitated.

"An idiot?" he suggested, since that was what her expression seemed to be saying.

She shook her head, and the scorn softened into something much more like pity. He wasn't sure he liked it better. "More like a wounded bear."

"A wounded bear," he repeated.

"Not to point out the obvious, dude, but Mom's death did a number on you. It wasn't your fault, you know."

What? "I never said it was."

Her gaze softened further. "No. But you've always *thought* it."

He was shaking his head, but the world was already tilting on its axis.

"You always make it about Dad. Dad not taking care of her, Dad not pulling his weight. But I saw you, Trey. I saw you trying to pick up the slack. Doing all the work in the yard. Around the house. Repairing, cleaning, trimming, tidying—fixing. Fixing fucking everything like if you just worked hard enough, you could *be* dad and take the weight off her."

It was a sneaker wave, what she'd said, the kind that crawled up the beach and snatched your feet out from under you. The kind that dragged you into a riptide.

He was still shaking his head.

"Trey. I *saw*. And then you did it again. To Karina. If you worked hard enough, if you built an empire that couldn't be touched, if you poured enough money into the life you were leading with her, nothing bad could ever happen to her."

"Except me," he said. "I happened to her."

Brynn glared at him.

"Mom loved Dad, you know. I mean, there's no accounting for taste, but she did. And the fact that he never had any money didn't bother her in the slightest. The thing that bothered her was the fact that he was so busy with all his scheming and risk-taking that he wasn't *there*. She just wanted him to be more present. And maybe if he had been—if he hadn't been so busy trying to *fix* everything—then he would have been able to really, well, *fix everything*.

"The only thing bad about you, Trey," Brynn said, tears filling her eyes, "is that you think we want what you can *give* us. You don't understand that what we want is *you*."

"But she doesn't," he insisted wildly, because his own eyes were filling with tears and he couldn't, *couldn't* cry—*hadn't*, not even when his mother had died. "She can't. Not after what I did. I almost took everything away from her."

Brynn sighed deeply. She brushed a hand over her eyes. "When she was yelling at you. Why do you think that was? Was it because she thought you were taking everything away from her?"

Was it? He heard the echo of Auburn's words, suddenly: Oh, my God, is that really how you see this? That this is all about you and what you did? Do you have any *idea what an asshole that makes you?*

He was starting to get the idea.

"You know what?" Brynn said. "Don't answer that. I know the answer. You know the answer. I don't want to play Socrates. Just —man the fuck up and figure it out."

A faint thread of hope, like the first strand in a new web, strung itself through him.

"How do I—how do I fix it?"

"Oh, God, Trey, you're *hopeless.*"

Which was funny because that little thread of hope was growing stronger every minute. Something he could hang onto.

Brynn shrugged. "If you were anyone else trying to win your woman back, I'd say you needed to make a grand gesture. Fly her to Paris, buy her a rock and get down on one knee. But in your case, you've got to quit showing love with money. You need to do something else. Something that speaks *her* language."

"So you're saying ... you're saying I need the opposite of a grand gesture. I need ..."

I deserve someone who treats me like a human being with free will—

He thought about it a moment, and then he knew. Not exactly what he was going to do, but the spirit he had to do it in. She'd showed him, after all, over and over again. She'd thought she was convincing him to love an inn, but in truth, she'd taught him much more than that. How a simple faith in community and friendship and family could buoy people up. How a little bit of space to breathe could make it so much easier to be human.

How small—sometimes tiny—acts of kindness and love made people's days or changed their lives.

"I need a humble gesture."

42

A uburn held a party at Beachcrest to celebrate its new ownership. Nothing big, but her siblings came, and several of her friends and acquaintances from town, and Brynn and Carl, of course, and the two romance writers who could make the trip—Deja and Aria. Auburn served champagne and lots and lots of homemade cookies, and the atmosphere was festive.

She stood on the sidelines. She was thrilled. Of course she was. But—

Chiara appeared at her side. "Great party," she said. She threw her arms around her sister.

"Thanks."

As she started to pull away, Chiara grabbed both her arms.

"Auburn."

She tried to look away, before tears could fill her eyes.

"You don't look like a woman who just got everything she ever wanted," Chiara whispered.

Auburn didn't bother trying to lie to her sister. It wasn't worth it. "I'm happy. Of course I'm happy. I love this place. And I know I will always love this place. But—"

Chiara waited. Patiently.

"It's stupid, I know it's stupid—"

"I doubt it," Chiara said.

"—but I wish he were here."

"He could be here," Chiara said quietly. "You could ask him to come."

Startled, Auburn looked at her sister. "And then what? And then every time he needs to feel like a man, every time he wants to call the shots, I just knuckle under and let him?"

"Is that what you did? You knuckled under?"

"No. No, I fought him—but—"

"That's right. You didn't knuckle under."

"But I did all those years with Patrick."

"Yes. You did. For a while. But in the end, you walked then, too, and that's what counts. Look what you've done. You've done exactly what you said you wanted to do, and you did it your way, in the best possible way, working with your community, bringing in all the people who cared to help you. You did it with so much strength and courage and—I'm so proud of you. They're proud of you, too. And grateful, Auburn. They're so grateful."

She made a sweeping gesture of the room. It encompassed everyone there, and all the ones that weren't, too. The friends who'd reunited and the lovers who'd found courage, the married couples who'd finally found the space and time to talk about what mattered.

Rick and Dewann.

Trey ... and Auburn.

Because he wasn't the only one Beachcrest had changed that week. It had changed her, too. It had proved to her that she was strong and brave and that no one, *no one* was going to take away what was hers.

"I got so angry," Auburn said quietly. "I was so angry at him."

"Of course you were," Chiara said. "You were scared. You were scared of being controlled, treated like a child, made small. But no one is ever going to do that to you again, Auburn. You know why not? Because you're never going to let them."

Auburn was crying, openly. She could see that some of the other guests at the party were eyeing her curiously, but she didn't care. She reached for a pile of cocktail napkins and mopped at her face, but it was a lost cause.

"I was never scared of him," she said wetly.

Chiara shook her head—agreement.

"I was scared of myself. That I wasn't strong enough to be with someone like him. Or maybe ... someone at all."

"But you don't have to be scared of that. You never have to be. You're the strongest person I know. Brave. Persistent. And look at you! You own your own inn."

"I do," Auburn said, a smile breaking through.

She just wished—

She wished he were here to celebrate it with her. Because maybe it was the stupidest thing she'd ever thought, but she believed there was at least a chance, a slim chance ... that he was the one person who loved Beachcrest as much as she did.

Although maybe ...

Maybe it wasn't Beachcrest he loved.

Maybe—he'd loved her.

And maybe he still did.

Because she still loved him.

And when she loved something, when she wanted something ...

She fucking did something about it.

43

"Beachcrest, Auburn speaking."

On the other end of the line, the caller took a deep breath. "I'd like to make a reservation."

Her heart pounded, because she knew that voice. Of course she did. She'd know it anywhere. It rumbled against her skin and ruffled the tiny hairs on her neck. It made her whole body sit up and take notice.

But she made herself be calm. And cool.

"Absolutely, sir. How can I help you?"

She hadn't expected to hear from him. It had been five days since the party, and she'd been busy with her own plans—so this was *unexpected*. She didn't know what it meant.

But she could hope.

"I'm taking some time off from business-building. To explore some other career options and just generally sort out my life. I've heard Beachcrest is a good place to do that."

Her heart was pounding now. Lungs squeezed. He wouldn't do this to tease. Couldn't. He had to mean it the way it sounded. "'Time off from business-building.' That sounds serious."

"It's like a really big vacation. For now. And rumor has it that

Beachcrest is the best place to take a vacation and figure things out."

His voice was low, warm, and it vibrated in all the places he'd touched with his hands, his mouth, his ....

"Yes. I can attest to the fact that that's true."

"Do you have any vacancies?"

Now he was just messing with her, a teasing turn on the word. And she loved it.

"We—let me just get into the computer." She opened the reservation screen, even though she knew. She knew the whole schedule by heart without looking, always.

"You're in luck. We had a cancellation yesterday, and we have one room available, for a week. The guest house room. You can view the room online if you want to see the details, but it has a queen bed in a standalone structure, with its own bath and its own gas fireplace. It's a lovely place for—*figuring things out*."

She heard his sharp inhale. "Sounds perfect for me."

"I'll put you in the computer, then. What—what will you be doing on your trip? Do you need us to make any dinner reservations for you? Or—we can do boat rentals, that kind of thing."

"I'm thinking about a very long beach walk," he said. "I don't suppose—no—I guess that wouldn't make any sense, would it? I don't suppose you do beach *tours*."

"You mean, have someone accompany you on this long beach walk? Point things out to you? Show you the sights?"

"Yes. That's what I was thinking. Maybe there could be a picnic. I've heard Tierney Bay Diner does really great takeout. I could order something, if the inn has a small cooler I could borrow..."

"Well," she said. "We aim to be a full-service operation. I don't see why we couldn't custom build that experience for you. A long beach walk. Did you know you can walk all the way from Tierney Bay to Hipsalu on the beach at low tide? And as luck would have it, there'll be a particularly low tide tomorrow. I could find someone to accompany you on your walk. It would take several hours, and that's without stopping for a picnic. If you took a picnic break, though, there's a spot I can recommend that's secluded. There's a little cave. If you brought a blanket to spread out ..."

He made a low sound at the other end of the phone, which vibrated in her belly.

"So," she said. "You're all set, then. When will you be checking in?"

She heard the front door open, and then he stepped into the front office, holding his cell phone. And she smiled. She couldn't have helped it if her life had depended on it. Because he was wearing board shorts and a Tierney Bay t-shirt and flipflops, and he had a towel slung over one arm and a bucket with a plastic shovel in it in his other hand. He saw her smile, and his own lit up his face.

"Auburn," he murmured. "I was wrong."

"Yes. You were an overassertive, presumptuous macho dipshit with a fix-it complex. But I also know you had your reasons."

He came up to the desk and set down his towel and shovel and pail. Leaned over the desk, rested his elbows on it. "You are the strongest woman I have ever met. And the most beautiful. I love the way you see the world. I love that you saw through me. I love—"

She couldn't catch her breath. The way he was looking at her made it impossible.

"I love *you*."

Her eyes filled with tears. She had to brush them back and find her ability to form words. "That's a pretty good speech."

"It's not a speech. It's the truth. I did have a whole speech, but I forgot it when I looked at you."

"Oh."

"It had something to do with—Brynn and I had a talk. About my mom. And how—"

His eyes were shiny.

"I'm not crying," he said. "Okay, maybe I'm sort of crying."

"I would be good with you crying," Auburn said. "I've heard this rumor that men do that now. It's not just for women anymore."

That made Trey laugh.

"Brynn says that I blame myself for my mom's death. I convinced myself that if I'd worked harder she wouldn't have had to work so hard ... I'm definitely crying," he said. "Shit, Auburn, I am not sure I can do this. It's so—*wet* and *gooey*."

She giggled. She reached under the desk and handed a tissue to him. He took it, looked down at it in mock confusion, then swept it across his brow and tried to stick it in his non-existent breast-pocket, handkerchief-style. She pulled it out again and gently dabbed at his eyes. He caught her hand, pulled her close, and kissed her until they were both breathless and panting.

"Stupid counter," Trey said to the obstacle between them. "Anyway, Brynn says—I should stop saying that, shouldn't I?"

"Yes."

"At some point, maybe it was when my mom died, I don't really know, I decided no one was ever going to suffer again because of a man's inadequacies," he said. "Karina. Carl. Brynn. You. I was going to take care of all of them. Everyone. With money. My way. And if there was someone I couldn't take care of properly, it meant I didn't deserve her." He took a deep breath. "I wish I could promise never to do it again, but you know how hard bad habits die."

"I do. Like my bad habit of assuming that if a man has a will as strong as mine—okay, *almost* as strong as mine—" she smirked at him "—he probably also wants to control me?"

"Like that."

"We could maybe make a pact. To not run away the next time we get scared or frustrated or feel like we aren't what the other person needs or the other person isn't what we need. We could just *talk about it.*"

"Yes. That sounds like an excellent plan. And that's a damn good thing, because I hated not being with you."

Now she was the one crying. "I hated not being with you, too."

"Can you—come out from behind that fucking desk?"

"Yes," she said, and did. And this time, when he kissed her, there was nothing between them.

When they broke apart, she said, "I need to show you something."

"Yeah," he said, dropping his gaze to where his board shorts revealed all. "Me too."

She swatted at him. "No. Seriously. Come with me. Wait, hang on."

She went behind the desk, fumbled for a moment, and came back around again. "This way."

He followed her out to the guest cottage. She unlocked the door and let him in.

"You put in a new desk!" he said. "With a built-in charging station."

"And I upgraded the Wi-Fi."

"Did you do this—?"

"I did it because you were right. It's time for a change, and it has been for a while. People want to sit down and answer emails and charge their devices, even when they're on vacation. But I also did it because ..."

She stopped, and looked up at him, all big blue eyes, wide and ... worried.

"I wanted you to be able to come here and work whenever you want." She took a deep breath. "If you want."

"You did this ... for me." He was filled with a bright, unfamiliar wonder. Of course, she was marvelous. He'd known all along. But this was different. This was *for him*.

When was the last time anyone had done anything for him?

When was the last time he'd wanted anyone to?

She reached into her pocket. "I made you a marketing postcard. I was going to send it. But I didn't get a chance."

It was a collage—a photo of Beachcrest, one of Breaker Rock, one of the whole beach. And the text said, "Come for the newly upgraded Wi-Fi, stay for the owner, who loves you."

He stared at it, warmth filling him up. Chasing away all the cold and numb spots.

"You—"

"I love you," she affirmed.

"Even though I wanted to tear down your inn? And even though I almost made you lose it? And even though I acted like an ass after I almost did?"

"And even though you have terrible taste in breakfast foods. And refuse the good things in life like hot dogs and marshmallows. And even though you spend way, way too much money on cologne."

"I got a new one. Because the old one seemed like it had some bad memories attached to it."

She stepped close, put her nose against his shirt, and inhaled deeply. "Ohhhhh," she said. "I'm a fan."

He couldn't help himself, he dipped his head and kissed her. Her mouth opened on a moan and her hands came up to clutch his head.

He was about to scoop her up and carry her to bed when she asked, "Are you really taking time off?"

He nodded. "Yeah. I want to do something different for a

while. Build physical things instead of businesses. There's nothing wrong with moving money around, if it brings you pleasure. But I don't do it because it brings me pleasure, I do it because I'm afraid of the alternative. And—that's not a good reason. What I loved most—when I was happiest—was when I was building things. Fixing things. Making things more beautiful. I stopped because I didn't believe I could be that man and also be the man Karina needed—"

Auburn was shaking her head. "You know you are already the man I need, right?" she asked. "I don't care what you do. You can move money or build and fix things. You can live in San Francisco or here. You can wear Armani and Versace or you can shop at Sea Stuff. None of that has any bearing on how I feel about you. Besides," she said. "I don't need you to take care of me."

He grinned at that. "No. You definitely don't." Then his expression grew serious. "Will you let me, though? Sometimes?"

She smiled. "Of course." She got up on tiptoes and whispered into his ear, her breath a thrill of sensation against his skin. "You could take care of me right now."

He growled. Scooped her up. Carried her across the room and deposited her on the bed. Climbed over her, bracing himself up on his arms and lowering his body so he could feel the whole length of hers. The softness of her curves and the heat between her legs—even through her leggings and his shorts.

"God, I missed you." He took her sweet, hot mouth, loving her taste, the little sounds she made as he swept his tongue in, the way she clutched at his clothing.

He paused only long enough to strip off her clothes, and his, and to find a condom. Then he knelt over her and did what he'd promised—he took care of her—of both of them, his blood rising like the highest of high tides, swelling his veins, his cock, his whole fucking universe. He guided himself to where her body was slick and ready for him. He slid home, watching his own progress on her face, the pink rising in her cheeks, the flare of her pupils, and then, as he pressed deep, the shadow of her lashes as her eyes fell closed and her lips parted.

She was alive and eager under him, bucking under the weight of his hips, meeting every one of his strokes with her own. Her tongue strained against his. She nipped his lower lip and he bit back, which made her cry out and fuck him harder. And at the end they raced each other over the edge, gazes locked. She wouldn't let him look away. He *couldn't* look away. He saw everything in her eyes. He watched the pink flood up her chest, over her throat, and when it reached her face, he watched her mouth fall open in surprise and pleasure. Nothing came out except a whisper. "Oh, fuck, Trey. Oh, *fuck*."

Then he lost himself completely in the intensity of his own climax. It was like getting pulled under by the surf, the waves so close together and each more potent than the last, until consciousness drowned in a sea of sensation.

They lay in each other's arms a long time afterwards. Until it was time to head down onto the beach to watch the sun set over the Pacific.

As dark fell, a few fireworks brightened the purpling sky. Auburn started to laugh.

"What?"

"Well. You may have spoken some bullshit in the course of our negotiations, but you can stand by at least one claim."

He cocked his head to one side. "Yeah, what's that?"

"You are good with giving the fireworks."

"Better than that?" He gestured at the one currently spilling gold shards over the Pacific.

When he turned to look at her, she was smiling, and by the

light of the fading sparkles, he could see the heat banked in her
gaze.

"Oh, yeah. So much better."

EPILOGUE

Three Months Later

The Romance Experience weekend was a blast. In the end, twelve guests met the threshold to win the experience, the four romance writers returned to host them, and almost everything went off without a hitch. The authors decided there should be two "tracks" in the experience weekend, one for guests who saw themselves purely as readers, and one for those who were aspiring writers—and the group split perfectly down the middle. The readers spent hours talking about their favorite books and characters, biking, hiking, and eating, while the writers spent those same hours in workshops—and everyone joined together for afternoon cookies and tea, evening campfires, and, of course, breakfast.

Auburn and Trey stood in the doorway of Beachcrest and waved goodbye to the last of the guests, all declaring they'd be back soon with their friends and families.

"I think that was a success," he said to her, smiling.

"It was pretty great."

"I think we should make it a yearly event."

"We?" she teased.

He'd been amazing this weekend—leading hikes and bike rides, building beach fires, frying bacon—and generally charming the crap out of their guests. He acted like he'd been made for the beach inn life, like there was nothing he'd rather do than carry towels and chip in to make up beds in a pinch.

"We," he said, nodding. "I want to ask you something."

His voice had gotten very serious, and she turned her undivided attention on him. After a weekend in which they'd been too busy even for a quickie, she was ready for some alone time with him tonight. He looked good enough to eat—hair longer now, and perpetually rumpled, eyes still as intense as the first time she'd found herself caught in his gaze, and a body that could fill out an expensive suit or stretch the confines of a soft cotton tee with equally breath-stopping results.

"Okay."

"When the sale of Home Base went through, even with all the debts, I made some money, as I told you."

"Yes."

"My original plan, before I met you, was to use most of that money to try to build to the next level."

"To get richer. Build bigger companies. Make sure you could buy all your relatives stuff they don't want."

He made a face at her. "Smartass. Yes. That was the old plan. But I've been so happy these last few months. Making Beachcrest stronger, sturdier, safer, more beautiful. With you. I want—I want to keep doing it. Building on what we've done so far. And that would be a hell of a lot easier if I weren't going back and forth between here and San Fran. If I were here —permanently."

Her breath stuttered in her chest.

"If that works for you, of course," he added. It was a tease, but also a question.

"That—works for me."

"I've been doing some research, and there's enough free land on this lot for another ADU. A little owner's cottage. I could build it. For you to live in. And if you were up for it, for—for us."

"Oh, Trey."

Her heart was so full, her chest ached.

"Is that a yes?"

"That's a yes."

He bent and kissed her.

"Marry that girl!" a voice called.

They laughed and broke apart. It was Carl—and that was his favorite line when he caught them in a public display of affection, however tame. He strode toward them now, cheerful and healthy—and a good twenty pounds slimmer than he'd been before his heart attack, thanks to a better diet and cycling with Trey on a gentle beachside path.

It had taken a while for Carl to forgive Trey for almost selling Beachcrest, but once he'd seen that Auburn held no grudge, he'd softened up, and before too long, the two men had started tackling overdue projects around the inn. Both Auburn and Trey made sure that Carl didn't take on anything *too* taxing—sometimes Mason or Levi would come over to help out if an additional share of brute strength was needed. Luckily for Trey, neither Mason nor Levi knew the whole story of how close Beachcrest had come to being lost. Someday, when they were both in extremely good moods, Auburn might tell them.

"Trey. This is the tile I chose for the new kitchen island. What do you think?"

Carl held up a piece of cobalt glass tile the exact color of Auburn's eyes.

"I think it's beautiful," Trey said. "But it's Auburn you have to ask. It's her inn."

She grinned at him. Half the time he forgot to ask her

approval himself, and they'd had a few all-out fights—including one in which she'd called him an alpha asshole with a control problem—but they'd also had some pretty epic makeup sex. She knew he respected her—and she also knew she was never going to let him get away with shit. Or—at least—she was going to dish out as much as he did.

"No one said anything to me about a new kitchen island," she said. "I'll have to think about that one for a few days."

"But—" Carl and Trey protested simultaneously, and Trey said, "We were going to get started on it today."

"Find something else to do. That front garden needs weeding pretty badly." Then she relented, laughing. "I'm just yanking your chains. The tile's gorgeous and that island is *crap*. Go to it. Just—I'm going to be making cookie dough later, so make sure I can still work in there."

When Carl had gone off with his piece of tile, she turned to Trey. "And? You have to let me photograph you working shirtless for the marketing materials for our next romance weekend."

He grinned at that. "Whose idea was that? No, wait, let me guess: Aria's."

She laughed and nodded.

He stepped toward her and gathered her into his arms. His breath brushed against her hair as he murmured, "You know I'll happily go shirtless for you any time, anywhere."

"You might want to experience Tierney Bay Beach in January before you make any promises you can't keep," she warned.

He laughed, and pressed her closer. "I'm not worried," he said. "I have beach magic to keep me warm."

"It doesn't work like that!" she protested.

"Oh, I think it does," he said, and bent and kissed her until they were both plenty warm.

ACKNOWLEDGMENTS

Thank you first and foremost to my readers — I am so grateful for you. You are why I do this. Also, to my reader-reviewers, who help other readers find the books of their hearts.

Thank you, thank you, thank you! to Sarah Murphy, the hardest-working and most supportive editor I know. You always see the book beneath the book—and know how to help me get there. It's a rare and special gift, and our collaboration is one of the great joys of my writing life.

I'm grateful for the sharp-eyed copyediting skills of Sarah Sarai. Sarah, it's been a pleasure working with you!

Thank you, Agent Emily, for always being there, hands-on or hands-off, whatever is called for at the moment. Love you.

Thank you, Peter Vessenes, for the eleventh-hour plot rescue and much-needed cup of tea. I hope I've done justice to your brilliant bit of setup, and if I've taken any absurd flights of fancy about what it's like to be a businessman, those are entirely my own.

Thank you, Dylann Crush, for being my inn expert (among other acts of helpful guidance). You steered me well, and any errors, inaccuracies, or bits of fictional goofiness are entirely my own.

Thank you, Rachel Grant, for all the love and support and plotting and walking, and especially for the many texts. I may not do explosions, but you helped me figure out the ticking time bomb!

Thank you to my other beta readers, all smart, lovely, and *loving* women: Christine D'Abo, Amber Belldene, and Karen Booth. You were super helpful with your comments, and you are always incredibly supportive and inspiring.

Writing is a solitary pursuit but never a lonely one. This book was made possible by the support and love of so many friends who persist in loving me no matter what kind of wacky author day I am having. Christine, Amber, Karen, and Rachel, always; the women of The Whole Package: Dylann, Christy Hovland, and Tamara Lush; The Effing Awesome Writer Chicks, including the aforementioned Rachel plus Kate Davies, Kim Fisk, Gwen Hayes, and Kris Kennedy; and the fabulous authors of the Corner of Smart & Sexy, including Karen plus Carolyn Hector, Ruby Lang, Susannah Nix, Reese Ryan, Teri Anne Stanley, and Maggie Wells.

Special thanks to Cheryl Cain, Molly Hays, Ellen Schroer, and Darya Swingle for countless acts of faith on an everyday basis.

And no set of acknowledgments would be complete without my mentioning Mr. Bell and the two not-so-little Bells, who are the best family anyone could ever ask for. I love you guys so much.

ALSO BY SERENA BELL

ABOUT THE AUTHOR

USA Today bestselling author Serena Bell writes contemporary romance with heat, heart, and humor. A former journalist, Serena has always believed that everyone has an amazing story to tell if you listen carefully, and you can often find her scribbling in her tiny garret office, mainlining chocolate and bringing to life the tales in her head.

Serena's books have earned many honors, including a RITA finalist spot, an RT Reviewers' Choice Award, Apple Books Best Book of the Month, and Amazon Best Book of the Year for Romance.

When not writing, Serena loves to spend time with her college-sweetheart husband and two hilarious kiddos—all of whom are incredibly tolerant not just of Serena's imaginary friends but also of how often she changes her hobbies and how passionately she embraces the new ones. These days, it's stand-up paddle boarding, board-gaming, meditation, and long walks with good friends.